"Even readers w]
will thoroughly enjoy
BURK PARSON ~~~~~, ~~ ~~~~~~ ~ ~~~~~~, ~~~~~
publishing officer, Ligonier Ministries; editor, *Tabletalk* Magazine

"Douglas Bond has done it again—a superb, gripping story based around the best-selling author of all time—John Bunyan. By using Bunyan's own words, setting them in historical context, and applying his love of the subject, Bond sets us firmly in 17th Century England. He weaves his story around the transformation of the tinker of Elstow in a highly accessible manner. A thoroughly good read which I highly recommend."
JOHN HINSON, Licensed Lay Minister, Elstow Abbey and Abbey tour guide

"In this exciting and moving book, Douglas Bond introduces readers to one of Christianity's great heroes. Written from the perspective of John Bunyan's rogue friend turned jailor, this lively story echoes with Bunyan's own words as he passed through many trials and temptations on his pilgrim way to the Celestial City."
DR. JOEL R. BEEKE, President, Puritan
Reformed Theological Seminary, Grand Rapids

"John Bunyan's 'Christian' lived a remarkable, grace-filled life of adventure. Christian's creator John Bunyan lived a remarkable, grace-filled life of adventure, too. You already know Christian, now read this cleverly crafted book by Douglas Bond to get to know his creator."
STEPHEN J. NICHOLS, President, Reformation Bible College; Chief Academic Officer, Ligonier Ministries

"Even the whirlwind changes of plague, war, catastrophe, and revolution cannot change a sinner. But behind this providence stands a never-changing God of grace. Douglas Bond takes us into the life of one unto whom this grace abounded to observe how it changes a man. A pleasant and profitable read for all."
JAMES HAKIM, pastor, Hopewell ARP Church, Culleoka, Tennessee

The Hobgoblins

A novel on John Bunyan

A Factual Fiction
Set at Elstow Abbey
by
Harry Wylie
A Fellow Rogue Corrupted
by the
Prince of Rogues
John Bunyan
in Our Youth

Also by Douglas Bond

Mr. Pipes and the British Hymn Makers
Mr. Pipes and Psalms and Hymns of the Reformation
Mr. Pipes Comes to America
The Accidental Voyage

Duncan's War
King's Arrow
Rebel's Keep

Guns of Thunder
Guns of the Lion
Guns of Providence

Hostage Lands
Hand of Vengeance
Hammer of the Huguenots
The Battle of Seattle
War in the Wasteland
The Resistance

STAND FAST In the Way of Truth
HOLD FAST In a Broken World

The Betrayal: A Novel on John Calvin
The Thunder: A Novel on John Knox
The Revolt: A Novel in Wycliffe's England
Luther in Love

The Mighty Weakness of John Knox
The Poetic Wonder of Isaac Watts

Augustus Toplady: Debtor to Mercy Alone
Girolamo Savonarola: Heart Aflame

Grace Works! (And Ways We Think It Doesn't)
God Sings! (And Ways We Think He Ought To)

God's Servant Job
The Truth About Ruth

The Hobgoblins

A novel on John Bunyan

DOUGLAS BOND

SCRIPTORIUM
PRESS

ISBN: 978-1-945062-13-1 (pbk)
ISBN: 978-1-945062-16-2 (ePub)

Cover designed by Robert Treskillard.

Printed in the United States of America

Library of Congress Cataloging-in-Publication Data

Bond, Douglas, 1958-
The Hobgoblins a novel on John Bunyan / Douglas Bond. – 1st
[edition].

pages cm

Summary: Written in the persona of Harry Wylie, companion of
the rebel John Bunyan, corrupted by the village blasphemer in his
youth, who gives his eyewitness version of the life of Bunyan, including
their service in the English Civil War, the various trials of Bunyan, and
his imprisonment, where Harry has become jailer; Harry believes
people never change, and Bunyan's principled stand against civil
tyranny he long dismisses as yet another expression of his rebellion.

ISBN: 978-1-945062-13-1 (pbk.)
1. John Bunyan--Juvenile fiction. 2. Religious liberty--History--17th
century--Fiction [1. English Civil War--History--17th century--Fiction. 2.
Stuart England--History--17th century--Fiction. 3. Courage in wartime--
Fiction. 4. Puritan--History--17th century--Fiction. 5. Christian apologetics-
-History--17th century--Fiction. 6..] I. Title.

BT761.3.B66 2020
234--dc23
                                                2013049333

For my beloved readers

"Hobgoblin nor foul fiend
Can daunt his spirit;
He knows he at the end
Shall life inherit!"

John Bunyan

"There was a young man in our town, to whom my heart was knit more than to any other, but he being a most wicked creature for cursing, and swearing, and whoring... I met him in a certain lane, and asked him how he did; he, after his old swearing and mad way, answered, he was well. 'But, Harry,' said I, 'why do you swear and curse thus? What will become of you, if you die in this condition?' He answered me in a great chafe, 'What would the devil do for company, if it were not for such as I am?'"

John Bunyan

"Some men by feigning words as dark as mine,
Make truth to spangle, and its rays to shine."

John Bunyan

"...I set pen to paper with delight,
And quickly had my thoughts in black and white;
For having now my method by the end,
Still as I pulled, it came; and so, I penned..."

John Bunyan

CONTENTS

1

Steepling Plunge

*L*ooking back, John Hinson, Licensed Lay Minister at historic Elstow Abbey, regretted a great deal about the 9th of April, in the year of our Lord, 2020. Springtime in middle England can come in like a runaway Thames barge, and in the early morning hours of April 9, 2020, it came in like an entire fleet of untethered barges.

Turning onto his right side, Hinson crammed the first knuckle of his right hand into his ear, a technique he had developed when his daughters were newborns. But the wind howled so relentlessly against the window in Hinson's bedroom that the technique was ineffectual in allowing him to sleep through the tempest. He lay blinking into the darkness, his wife breathing steadily and quietly at his side.

How does she do that? mused Hinson.

It would not be precisely accurate to say that Hinson had a strong aversion to storms. More accurate it would be to say that he had an unhinged terror of the phenomenon. To him, howling wind and pounding rain were not events of the natural order of things, the mere convergence of warm air and cool, or the uncalculated rising and falling of barometric pressure. For Hinson, storms were more in the category of hobgoblins and foul fiends, as someone once put it, with insatiable will, unbridled force, and malevolent intent.

Hinson took storms personally. He firmly believed they were evil, wholly unassuaged by the mere wreaking of random damage and mayhem. They were meteorological smart bombs, intent on the precise and unmitigated annihilation of John Hinson, Licensed Lay Minister of Elstow Abbey. With Hinson, this was a deep conviction, the fortieth article of faith.

And then there was the matter of the time of day, or, rather, the time of night.

Hinson felt his body shudder in the bedsheets. To say that he was afraid of the dark was not strictly accurate. It was a profoundly inadequate proportional inaccuracy. For Hinson, storms and the dark—he would prefer to have raw flesh torn slowly from his back, and a benevolent burning at the stake—any torment was better than facing off with storms in the dark. The bedroom window rattled mockingly with the next gust.

His wife's breathing remained deep and steady at his side. In the ghostly blue dimness of the nightlight, he observed her eyes gently closed, a peaceful smile playing on the corners of her lips.

His discomfort momentarily suspended, Hinson mused yet again on the wonder of how on earth she did it. Then, eyes goggling the darkness, he pulled the bedsheet up more tightly under his chin.

And then another thought occurred to him. What would become of his beloved abbey? *His* abbey. That's how he often thought of it. He tried consoling himself with the fact that the massive stone edifice had managed to remain erect through nearly 900 unruly spring storms. Surely it would merely shake itself and hurl a defiant guffaw at this one. Grabbing a fistful of duvet, Hinson sank his teeth into the wad, and flailed over onto his left side. His abbey would remain defiant. Surely it would.

At the first pale hint of morning, Hinson staggered from his bed, splashed water onto his face, dressed and wrapped himself in his Macintosh. He would have a cup of Typhoo when he returned, drink the whole pot of it, if all was well.

Bracing himself against the wind, he breathed a sigh of relief at sight of his Citroën Picasso; his beloved, red Citroën Picasso. At least it had survived the fury of the storm. After fumbling yet again for his key, he tapped his forehead, and pressed the ignition button. Hinson was old-school and, though he had owned his Citroën Picasso for one month short of two years, he still found himself fumbling for the key and the ignition into which one put one's car key—as one properly used to do so.

The French vehicle had not been engineered for storms any more than Hinson had been. Like a tempest-tossed vessel in a gale, his seven-seater car rocked with each new gust of wind as he piloted it onto Ampthill Road. Swerving to avoid branches and debris scudding across the road, Hinson gripped the steering wheel until he lost feeling in his fingers. An especially strong gust hit the vehicle broadside as he maneuvered onto the High Street. Prudently, Hinson removed his foot from the gas pedal and covered the brake.

Hinson glanced through the windscreen, wiper blades doing their best to sploosh a path in the rain. The Jetty archway into the old coaching inn still stood, its black timbers straining under the load as they had for ages. Leaning every direction of the compass over the High Street, the row of half-timbered cottages had managed to weather the storm. It was a marvel that Bunyan's Mead still stood. The Leaning Tower of Pisa had nothing on Bunyan's Mead. Looking like an old man hunched over his Zimmer frame, or several old men, cheek-by-jowl, bracing themselves with their walkers against the wind, this quaint cluster of white-washed and black-timbered houses had bested the thermodynamics of entropy for centuries, long before John Bunyan's day.

"Bravo, gentlemen, still standing today," murmured Hinson as he slowed to negotiate the turn onto the one-lane track called Church End.

With a nod toward the brick and half-timbered structure on his right, Hinson murmured, "Well done, Moot Hall, sturdy fellow."

Branches littered the single track as he drove slowly along the stone wall bordering the churchyard. He bent and looked across the passenger seat on his left as he drove. The ancient abbey was visible in snatches through the majestic old stand of horse-chestnut trees that rose protectively over the rows of tombstones in the ancient churchyard.

14

He breathed a sigh of relief. "You've done it again, old girl," said Hinson. "It's been nigh on 900 years. One does wonder just how many of these you've managed to weather."

The village green on his right, Hinson turned left at the end of the stone wall encircling the cemetery. There in front of him was the 13th century bell tower.

Hinson frowned. Something wasn't right. Guiding the Citroën Picasso into a parking space near the gate, he opened the door. A sudden gust of wind nearly wrenched the door from its hinges. Clutching his Macintosh about his collar, his head down against the wind, Hinson battled manfully into the breach and through the gate.

The horse-chestnut trees in the cemetery creaked and groaned as they were pummeled by the howling winds. How they remained standing was a wonder. Hinson saw that some branches had cracked under the strain and littered the churchyard; one great branch lay far too close to the gravestone marking where John Bunyan's mother Margaret and sister, of the same name, had been laid to rest in 1644.

Hinson shook his head sadly. It was a shame for a piece of antiquity to fall under the indiscriminate caprice of a Bedfordshire spring storm. How he hated storms.

But when he rounded the base of the bell tower, he halted in his tracks, the wind launching his hair into a vertical coiffure and snapping petulantly in the skirts of his Macintosh.

"Oh, no! This is not good!" He could not believe his eyes. A branch from a horse-chestnut tree, thicker than a man's thigh, had cracked under the strain of the wind, but only partially. It was still connected to the main trunk of the great old tree, but its outer limb had fallen against the tower. It appeared to be lodged in a notch of the crenellation that had been guarding the top of the edifice for the last 800 years.

"This is really not good," observed Hinson, pulling out his mobile phone. He attempted to open it, then remembered that one did not need to open mobile phones anymore. They came ready opened.

Dismissing a "Low battery" notification with an impatient swipe and an eloquent *humph*, Hinson scrolled through his favorites and tapped to connect to the vicar. He'd start with the vicar, then call the village council to get a maintenance crew on site as soon as possible.

Holding his mobile up to his right ear, he surveyed the damage. There was no way workmen could safely remove the massive branch, not until this wind died down; even then it would be tricky business. How long he had been holding his mobile to his ear, Hinson was not sure. Pulling it away, he scowled at the device. Looking at the upper left corner of the screen, he read, "No service."

"Of course not." He nodded knowingly. "Not in this weather."

Hinson was not a man to be so easily put off. Something needed to be done. Reaching inside his Macintosh he pulled out a giant skeleton key. Thrusting it into the ancient lock on the door at the base of the tower, he turned the key. The latch replied with a *clunk*.

Once inside the tower, he turned around, wedging his backside against the oak door; breathing heavily, one backward step at a time, he walked the door closed against the wind. *Clunk!*

Hinson suddenly found himself in the relative silence of the interior of the ancient tower, the air musty with age. Outside, the storm raged on, though muffled by the thickness of the walls. Inside, it was pitchy dark.

Fumbling with his phone, Hinson tried to recall what his daughter had told him. "Just swipe up, Aged P. It's really quite simple. Then tap on the torch icon, just there. Voila! You need never be without a torch again."

After several moments, a pin-prick of white light struck in his eyes. "Clever girl," he murmured, blinking rapidly. He felt an instant of foreboding. "What's this? 'Low battery.' Dashed, newfangled piece of rubbish." He would need to hurry.

Cautiously he mounted the narrow circular stairway. Hinson was not a small man. He liked to think of it as all muscle, as it once had been. But whatever one called it, he found it rubbing on both sides of the narrow column around which the stairs climbed up past the bells.

The bells. Several of them had been there for over 400 years. One was called Bunyan Bell because the ornery tinker John Bunyan in his youth used to take great delight in ringing that particular bell, often and especially when it was not supposed to be rung. Hinson liked the ruffian tinker and felt a certain affinity with the rags-to-riches peasant, though the fellow never achieved anything like riches, a certain notoriety, but no riches. Far from it. But it was something of a feather in the cap of otherwise grandly insignificant Elstow to have been the place that suckled the best-selling author of all time.

Amidst these reflections, Hinson mounted the treads inside an ancient stone stairwell, far too narrow for his liking. Sweat formed on his brow, and he heard his own breathing competing with the muffled winds pummeling the tower outside. The treads were steep and irregular, and the torch on his mobile was wholly inadequate for dispelling the kind of darkness that reigned within the decaying vascular system of that ancient edifice.

More than once, miscalculating the rise of the next tread, Hinson stubbed his toe on the hard stone. Making it still more difficult to calculate, the treads were worn down in the middle by the centuries of feet that had trodden upon them. The dip in the middle was several inches lower than the less-traveled edges of the stone steps. Making matters worse, little fragments of stone littered each tread and acted like ball bearings underfoot. Clinging with his fingers onto the cold stones of the rounded walls of the stairwell, careless of his discomforts, Hinson climbed still higher.

"Even in matters of courage," he murmured to himself, his words quavering warily back at him from the stone tower, "one must be cautious."

His phone vibrated. He steadied himself, glancing at the screen. Perhaps it was the vicar. "Dash it all. Another notification. 'Battery low.'" Across from where it said, "No signal," Hinson saw the battery charge indicator sneering at him; "2%," it taunted.

"That's, not good." But surely, he reasoned, he was closer to the top than to the bottom. Fortifying himself with a lyrical fragment from the tinker, "'The hill though high I covet to ascend,' and what not," Hinson flicked a stone ball bearing aside with his toe, and resumed his intrepid ascent of the tower.

Hinson would never be sure exactly how near he had climbed to the doorway opening onto the lead roof of the tower. It would only be some time later that he would remember much else about the events that immediately transpired.

Firstly, his torch died. Hinson found himself in utter darkness. The storm outside seemed to intensify in that darkness. He considered halting, turning about face, and making his way down the ancient stone staircase. But Hinson was not a man so easily dissuaded from his duty; besides, somehow the prospect of climbing down seemed more perilous in the dark than climbing up.

Without his torch, it was impossible to inspect the condition of the next tread. Groping with his hands, Hinson placed a tentative shoe on the next stair. As he shifted his girth onto the uphill foot, things began going downhill, rapidly so.

The stone ball bearings did their job. Clutching for a handhold, he heard his mobile clattering down beneath him, and wondered for a split second how much it would cost to repair or replace the wholly unreliable device. But in that split second, he, John Hinson, Licensed Lay Minister of Elstow Abbey, began his steepling plunge. He felt he was irreplaceable—and hoped his wife and daughters agreed—but what of the repair? What would be the cost of said repair to his body and bones?

19

Instinctively Hinson spread his feet to try and halt the acceleration of his fall with friction against the circular stones lining the stairwell. He would later recall his left foot colliding violently with a protruding stone. But gravity had begun its unremitting work, mercilessly plunging his body and bones into the blackness.

It was when his chin first struck hard on a stone tread that Hinson began to wonder if repair would even be an option. Then, for a horrifying instant, he felt himself beginning to topple over into a backward, cartwheeling maneuver. Falling feetfirst seemed a far better option than hurtling backwards and headfirst into the abyss. Such a fall would most certainly be fatal. With the last ounce of his strength, in a corrective effort, he lunged forward. It would be one of the last clear memories for some time.

With a sickening thud, Hinson felt his forehead collide with the edge of an ancient cut stone. Don McLean's haunting melody "Starry, Starry Night," sprang instantly to his mind, or what was left of it. Hinson reached for the stars; it was as if he had become Vincent Van Gogh and was seeing the song unfold before his terrified eyes.

But then, one by one, each star fizzled and died. He had only thought he was in blackness before. He was about to discover that there is a total blackness that occurs that is far deeper than the mere absence of light. It was that total blackness now that enshrouded Licensed Lay Minister John Hinson in its greedy orifice.

2

Discovery

H ow are we feeling today?"

Hinson felt his eyeballs pop open. Clutching a fistful of bedsheet, he looked warily about the room.

"I said, how are we feeling today, Mr. Hinson?" It was the cheery voice of a middle-aged woman all in white. He watched as she pulled aside the drapes. A shaft of morning sunlight bolted into the hospital room.

Blinking rapidly at the light, Hinson lifted his left hand and gingerly touched his head. Bandages, thick wrappings of cotton bandaging where his head ought to have been; was he from Kandahar or Hounslow? He couldn't be sure which. Investigating the body that lay on the bed, he saw a leg encased in plaster, and held aloft by a traction device that looked like a davit on a fishing boat; the leg appeared to be the night's catch being yarded onboard the vessel. The catch wiggled its toes.

The woman in white hummed as she tidied the room; the shaft of sunlight illuminating her hair seemed to be passing through her white garments. Hinson felt his mouth restructuring itself into a large O, his eyes splaying into much the same shape.

"Hath it come, then?" He swallowed hard. "A-art thou? I-is this… is this it, then?"

She laughed. "Don't be silly! You asked me that same thing yesterday, and the day before that, and the day before that." She laughed again. "I'm not an angel—ask my mum. And this is not heaven. And you, Mr. Hinson, are very much still in the land of the living. Now, how about that cup of tea?"

"Tea? Dost thou have Typhoo?" asked Hinson, passing a hand across his eyes, a bewildered faraway expression on his features. "Doth I like tea?"

"Dear Aged P, of course you like tea, very much indeed." A young woman had just entered the room. "Much the same, Nurse?" she murmured.

"He's talking," replied the nurse in a whisper, "though a touch oddly, as if from the pages of Shakespeare or the King James."

"Tea it is, then, Aged P," said his daughter. "But nobody likes drinking tea on its own. I've brought you shortbread, my homemade shortbread. There's really none like it, so you've always said."

"Art thou speaking in rhyme for a reason?" asked Hinson. "Thou hast called me 'Aged P,' thou hast. But the shining one, she waketh me every morning and calleth me Hinson, or something. Dost I know thee?"

"Of course, you do," said his daughter. "Don't be silly. Aged P stands for Aged Parent. I am your daughter, silly, your favorite daughter, I might add."

"Hinson, Silly, Aged Parent—who am I?"

"Now, don't let's go and get all philosophical about it, Aged P. Drink your tea, white with two lumps of sugar."

Hinson scowled deeply and recoiled from the offered teacup. "But didst not I give up sugar for Lent?"

The nurse turned, raised her eyebrows, and nodded encouragingly at his words, quaint though they were.

"Yes, you did," replied Hinson's daughter. "But don't you remember, just like last year, and the year before, you gave up the giving up of sugar in your tea. 'Double self-denial' you called it. Just as two negatives make a positive, so two denials make an indulgence."

Hinson blinked rapidly.

"The operative word here, is 'remember,'" said the nurse. "This is all very encouraging. Though, mind you, there could be setbacks. Do you remember anything else?"

Hinson sipped his Typhoo pensively. "How hath I come by that?" he asked, staring hard at his left leg.

His daughter set her teacup down, and leaned closer to him. "That's where the mystery comes in," she said with a wink. "In your fall—"

"I do beg thy pardon, but, a fall? How hath I thusly fallen?"

"Just a wee one, nothing much, really. Well, actually it was a bit more than nothing much. That is to say, yes, well, you did have a bit of a tumble. In the tower, the morning of the big storm," she explained, with an

23

upward lilt in her tone as if inviting him to remember. She hesitated, looking at the nurse for support.

"Tower, prodigious tempest," murmured Hinson, stroking his beard in thought. "Wouldst thou be so kind as to plug in my mobile?"

Nurse nodded approvingly at his words.

"Yes, well, the exciting part about it all," continued his daughter, "is what you unearthed in the fall, the tumble, the little slippage, whatever you want to call it."

"Unearthed?" said Hinson. "Is that akin to exhumed?"

"No, nothing like," laughed his daughter. "Well, I suppose in a manner of speaking, yes. But the point is, as you fell, your foot, or something, must have dislodged a stone."

"Which foot, pray tell?"

"The one just there," said his daughter, pointing sideways at the plaster-encased leg.

"Doctor believes," interjected the nurse, "it's how you came to fracture your leg, your foot, your ankle— really, all of the above. Rather nasty fracture, it was— is."

"But, Aged P," continued his daughter, "you exhumed a treasure. That is, we hope it is a treasure."

"Treasure?"

"A box, a metal one," she said, "a sort of flattish one, like a notebook."

"Thou hast this box?" asked Hinson, setting his teacup on the side table. "Bring it me, forthwith."

"Nurse, might I have a moment with my father— alone?"

After the nurse left the room, his daughter's eyes sparkled and she mouthed her words conspiratorially. "I have it here, in my satchel." She drew it out and handed it to her father. "Aged P, more than anyone, you know the abbey and everything about its history."

"Dost I?"

"Of course, you do! Better than anyone. You know you do. Have you ever seen anything like it?"

Turning the tin box slowly in his hands, Hinson studied it. He ran his fingers along a neat row of rivets that attached the lid to the rest of the box.

"Well?" said his daughter. "Is it real?"

"Real?"

"I mean, it's not a hoax or a prank? Tell me it's not. It's really old, truly so, isn't it?"

"My spectacles, if you please," said Hinson, wincing as he sat up in the bed, his daughter positioning pillows to make him more comfortable.

"Well?" she urged.

"It might, perhaps, be both," he said, looking over his glasses at her.

"How could it be both? It's either ancient, or a hoax or prank."

For the first time since his tumble, Hinson laughed. Not a full-bodied guffaw, but something more than a mere smile. Another encouraging sign.

"It doth be most definitely old, my dearest," said Hinson. "But this doth be Bedfordshire, tin-worker Bunyan's country, and he wast ever a rogue for a jolly prank. So, its being old doth not necessarily mean it is not simultaneously a prank."

Hinson's daughter looked confused. "How doth—I mean—how does one find out?" she asked, nodding sideways at the closed door, "without letting, you know, word get out? I mean, if it is treasure, and all that," she waggled her head side-to-side, "it belongs to the one who exhumed it, so it would stand to reason?"

"Treasure or rubbish, we shalt never know what lieth inside," said Hinson simply, "until we hath opened it."

"But how?"

"My breakfast arriveth momentarily," said Hinson. "Whilst I consume it, thy job wilt be to go find me a stout hammer. Thou knowest what a hammer is, dearest one? One lieth snuggly in the boot of my Picasso. Bring it me, posthaste!"

3

Tin Treasure

W e can't simply bash the thing to pieces," said Hinson's daughter, moments later after returning to his bedside. Frowning at the hammer, she turned it this way and that. "What do you propose to do with a hammer?"

Hinson's brow furrowed. "Indeed, if it doth be a treasure, and we indiscriminately basheth said treasure with said hammer—"

"We destroy the treasure," his daughter finished for him. She turned the tin box so the full sunlight fell on the rivets. "Hello. It's aluminium, don't you think, Aged P?"

"Indeed."

"Like what fish come in?"

"Indeed."

"Well, then," she said. "I just might have a better idea."

Half an hour later she returned waving a can opener triumphantly. "We'll open the thing as if it were a tin of fish. No bashing needed."

And so, they did.

To say that Hinson's daughter was disappointed with the contents, would be an understatement akin to saying the House of Windsor, the Queen, the Crown Jewels, and all the obligatory regalia, had only slight influence on international tourism in the United Kingdom.

"Rubbish," she snorted. "Just a pile of old paper, with some scribbles here and there. Oh, and I had so hoped it was a treasure."

Hinson looked reprovingly at his daughter. "Thou art overhasty, my dearest. One knoweth not if it be treasure or rubbish lest one readeth what lieth, forthwith, therein, upon the parchment, thereupon."

"Read it? You want me to read it aloud?"

He nodded. "Indeed. Forthwith. Give it tongue."

4

Rebel Madman

Draining her teacup, Hinson's daughter cleared her throat and commenced reading:

The Hobgoblins of John Bunyan, penned by Harry Wylie, a fellow vulgarian corrupted in my youth by the very prince of rogues himself.

It was when first I heard that my old childhood companion was writing an autobiography of his life and times, I say, it was upon hearing this news noised abroad in our community that I determined to best him by crafting this my memoir of our mayhem and trickeries. I did not trust him fully to expostulate on the more colorful bits, hence, my determination to set pen to paper, and give it off in black and white.

Though there are other episodes I could include, I have chosen to commence the real story of the rebel madman John Bunyan in April of 1640, or it may have been 1641. My memory takes me back to the boggy slough between Harrowden, the hamlet of our births, and the nearby village of Elstow.

It was a beautiful, spring morning. The larks were singing in the woodland along the east side of the slough. The air was scented with pale-yellow primroses that grew in clumps of puckered leaves along the marshy banks of the slough. And the down-turned, purple-checked blossoms of snake's head fritillary bobbed on their stems along the hedgerow.

The morning sunlight was flashing through the branches of the trees, the tender green leaves just beginning to unfurl themselves as if emerald harbingers of the new season. An occasional breeze made the new leaves to flicker as the sun shone through the translucent green, nodding in the light air above us.

I breathed deeply of the mingling aromas of that fine morning. A perfect day for boys seeking adventure. We were, as was our custom, sniffing for mischief along the ditches and hedges of Bedfordshire. And mischief did we find that day—or, rather, it found us.

John Bunyan was in the lead. John was always in the lead. We had made our way to where the highway ran alongside the slough when adventure seized upon us. Just as we mounted onto the mud and earth of the highway, John made a halt in his tracks, his hand signaling for me to halt in mine. Which I did.

Now, I assumed he was just funning. Ours was an ordinary part of England. Mundane middle England, it was. In my short years of life very little of interest had occurred, at least not that I had been anything like aware of. No wars. No rumors of wars. Precious few public hangings. No pestilence, plague, or pandemic to give spice to our mundane existence. I believe we boys longed for a roaring good disaster to come along. Life would be so much more interesting if there were scheduled calamities making their soirees into our drab life, now and again. Or so we imagined. Little did we know then what cataclysmic misfortunes were in store in our futures.

I watched as John raised his stick. We were great ones for sticks, never venturing far without one firmly in hand, were we. And then he brought his stick down with a woosh and a crack on a hard-packed rut of the highway.

"Take that, you she-devil!" he shouted in triumph.

I bolted to his side. Then hastily took a step backward, the flesh beginning its crawling along my spine and neck. I felt my hair scrambling to stand upon its ends along my scalp.

"Th-that be an adder, John!" I cried.

He gave me a withering look. John was a great one for withering looks, and I so dreaded those looks. "What do you take me for, Harry? I know what it is."

"A p-poison adder, it be."

Another withering look. "Where's the larks in it, Harry, tell me, if she had no poison in them fangs of hers?"

"H-hers? How can you be so sure she's a she?"

He turned his back on the stunned adder, and, looking full on me, commenced a viperous anatomy lesson. "*Vipera berus*," he intoned, in what must have been his notion of how a Cambridge don might deliver a lecture. "You will observe, Harry, good fellow, that this adder is brownish in color, is she not?"

I stared at the adder behind him and nodded.

"And has zig-zagging patterns in dark brown running along her serpentine body."

Again, I nodded in the affirmative.

"Contrariwise, if she was not a she and was a he-adder, the brown would be pale gray, even black, and there'd be an inverted V on the back of his head, if she were a he, that is, and not a she."

While he had been expostulating on adders, I had not taken my eyes off the prone specimen behind him.

"Moreover, if this she-adder felt the need and struck—" Here he broke off, suddenly, and lunged at me. My heart nearly stopped, and I cried aloud.

After recovering from a laughing fit that I felt went on far longer than was proportional to its cause, he cleared his throat, jutted his chin, and recommended his tutorial on adders.

"That is to say, if this she-adder felt the need and struck her victim, there would, forthwith, commence extensive swelling, extreme discomfort, blistering, and the process of putrification, sometimes called gangrene, in the damaged tissue in the area around the bite. Concurrently, there would be drooping of the eyelids—" He paused to demonstrate said drooping in a most unnecessarily grotesque manner. "Numbness radiating throughout the body, eventually leading to paralysis of the organs, constricting of the throat, inability to breathe, gasping and clutching, and—"

He paused. I knew it to be for dramatic effect. He was a madman, but, unlike some, he was a predictable madman.

"*Death!*" his voice quavering in an unnerving manner as he intoned the dreadful word.

Throughout the duration of his discourse, John had his back to the adder, a creature that he must have assumed he had either stunned or killed altogether. My eyes grew wide as I watched the creature behind him begin stirring. First, its lower half twitched, but in an instant, its scaly head and beady eyes began oscillating.

"Take heed!" I managed to cry, in spite of the cold fingers that seemed to have laid fast hold about my throat. "She lives!"

My companion spun around on his heel just as the adder readied herself to strike. I was sickened at her slithering movement and unblinking, orange eyes.

I felt sure there was no escape for him. The she-adder was too close. As she cocked her body and made to strike, John reacted unlike how any ordinary human being would react. I felt sure of it.

Crying with glee, John fended her off as if his stick was a quarterstaff and she his tournament opponent. Just when I thought he was about to meet his miserable end, my sentiments underwent a shift. I began to pity the snake.

Somehow, in the flurry of stick, and snake, and boy, John managed to get a grip with his left hand around the adder's neck, her mouth wide, forked tongue frantically darting, her fangs dripping venom.

Humiliating as it is to confess, I felt my knees trembling underneath me; the shutters began closing in upon my eyes, my whole body feeling light as a feather, as if readying for a swoon. Though I despised myself for my inclination to swoon at times such as these, try as I might, I was utterly powerless to control the enervating phenomenon.

Meanwhile, John continued subduing the adder. Propping her fangs open with his stick, laughing uproariously all the while as if it were all merely an innocent game of tip-cat, he reached deep inside the condemned creature's mouth, back between her beady eyes, and, with a flourish, pulled out her venom sac with his bare fingers.

After which, he commenced a frenzied dance, spinning the hapless adder by the tail, slamming her head in the road ruts, then against a tree trunk, then skipping rope with her as he cavorted and gyrated in his vulgar rendition of a Whitsun Morris dance with an adder, now very much a dead adder.

Did I mention his singing? John fancied himself a master poet to rival the Bard of Stratford, did he. Throughout his wild cavort, he sang; profane and blasphemous was this singing. He prided himself on what he believed to be his ability to create words and music on the very instant, words he felt confident matched perfectly the particulars of the prank or caper just accomplished. Occasional poetry, he termed it, the very latest in the lyrical art, so he claimed. In the interest of avoiding bringing further condemnation down upon my own head, I, herein, record the lesser-profane fragments from this his serpent song, as he called it:

Thou slithering one, O creeping sight,
Art silent now under thy hellish plight;
Thou thought thy name would me survive
But I'm alive! O, I'm alive!

At the refrain, of which he seemed particularly proud, he would hurl the adder's body into the heavens, then catch it as it fell, and sing and dance some more.

Did I not say he was a very madman? Convinced that men do not change, my formative years spent with John Bunyan deepened my adherence to the unalterable dictum: Once a madman, always a madman.

5

Nocturnal Plunge

L
est my reader imagine I have selected the
worst behavior to represent the whole of the
man, indulge me as I relate yet another
significant incident from our youth.

"Hist, hist!"

I awoke with a start at the sound. A shaft of
moonlight shone on the hard-packed earth floor of
our hovel. I heard the steady breathing of my mother,
father, and siblings—and the scritch-scratching of
rats in the thatch overhead. It came again, more
persistently.

"Hist, hist!"

Silhouetted by the moonlight in the only window
in our cottage, was the head and shoulders of a
human person. I was relieved at that fact. Rubbing
sleep from my eyes with my fists, upon further

scrutiny, I recognized the stout features, broad shoulders, and unkempt hair of the silhouette. I arranged my bedclothes to look as if I were still under them—this was not our first nighttime adventure. Tip-toeing to the door, I grimaced as I lifted the latch, and slowly closed the door behind me. Who knew what the madman had in store for this night?

Without a word, I followed John past the half dozen cottages that made up the hamlet of Harrowden. My heart nearly ceased its pounding at the low growl of a cur. But I had no need of fear. John had made it his business to seduce all the dogs in our hamlet. It was part of his larger scheme to master our destinies at whatever time of day or night we pleased. Mind you, he had no special affection for canine creatures. I am not certain he had any special affection for any creature, save John Bunyan himself. But feigning kindness to the local curs meant freedom for us on our nighttime soirees. He termed it "an investment in our emancipation," did he.

The cluster of cottages now behind us, we struck out on the Bedford Road toward the river. He seldom informed me what our caper would be, and I was content, fool that I was, to follow his boundless and roguish imagination wherever it led us. This night, like so many before and after, would make me resolve to stop doing so; yet, here I was, doing so, yet again.

He had chosen the night well. The moon was bright, casting shadows from the clutching branches of horse-chestnut trees along the road, but illuminating our path in eerie blue light. John could be dull and lazy at will, but not when driven by the eager anticipation of an escapade.

37

We dog-trotted on the road that night, encountering no one. No one, that is, but the cheery conversation of thousands of frogs along the slough that bordered southwest of Elstow Abbey. Moonlight sparkled on the stained glass and glowed on the chiseled sandstone of the ancient abbey church. With dread, I followed John as he vaulted over the stone enclosure surrounding the churchyard.

We now moved amongst great vertical slabs of stone, many of them taller than I, the rigid markers of the dead. My breath came in hot blasts, my throat constricted, and I felt a greater thundering in my breast than the level of exertion required. I knew that John took a positive pleasure in passing through the burial grounds of the ancient dead, a positive pleasure in what he knew to be its horrifying effect upon me. He halted at the base of the 13th century bell tower and turned. The moonlight shone brightly on his grinning features, so brightly I could discern the clustered archipelagoes of his freckles.

"Shall we?" said he, gesturing with a sideways nod of his head at the great oak door of the tower.

John loved bells, loved ringing the bells. But unlike normal people, bell ringing types, he preferred to ring them at wrong times, and in patterns that sent false signals throughout the community.

I shook my head in wonder at him. Yet, here I was at his side, fellow ne'er-do-well in crime. John took pride in one of our bell-ringing, midnight exploits, during which he managed to call all Elstow to arms against a foreign invader. As if the Norman Conquest was being reenacted on the village green. On another occasion, he managed to affect a bell ringing pattern that strongly insinuated a somber tolling for the decease of the mayor, who was yet very much alive—and infuriated—upon hearing the news.

"Ah, ha, Harry, I can see it in your eyes," said he. "I know you want to. But we must away. We have this night, as they say, bigger fish to fry, my boy—or ought I to say, bigger eels to harvest." And then he winked knowingly at his words.

I did not know precisely what this meant, but secretly, I was relieved. Unlike John, I felt less pleasure than he in awakening the entire community on a false pretense, and in the middle of their night's sleep, to the rude and penetrating clanging of giant bells.

Leaving the abbey, its bell tower, its ancient bones, and secrets behind, I followed him, as near as I could determine in the dark, north by east, toward the river. At one point the moon went behind a cloud, and we found ourselves surrounded by pitchy darkness.

It was the smell that acted as a first warning. We were trespassing on a farmer's pasture when the moon departed. I held my hands before me as we walked. I could just barely make out John's movements ahead of me and to my left.

Suddenly, my foot struck something large—large, hot, hairy, and breathing, all of which I felt as I tumbled forward onto the massive body of a slumbering cow. More accurately, a formerly slumbering cow. My collision with its body rendered it no longer slumbering. And, as I was on the instant to learn, it was not a cow. It was a bull. Large and irrationally unhappy about being awakened from his beloved sleep, was he. As I ran for my life, thundering hooves churning the turf behind me, I stumbled over several other sleeping bovine. Bull or cow, I did not wait to discover. Scrambling to my feet, I made for the gate and safety. John thought it rousingly amusing and merely a prelude to our adventure.

The moonlight returned, and we carried on toward the river. After another quarter of an hour or so, John flopped into the reedy grass at the base of a giant willow tree, and I after him.

It was all madness, of course, but here I was not even knowing what was afoot. Whatever it was, we could not have asked for a more beautiful night for a caper. Moonlight shimmered on the ripples of the River Great Ouse making its winding way to the North Sea. Coots nesting along the banks gave off their soft rhythmic *chip, chip, chip* murmuring. In spite of our intrusion, myriad frogs, content with their world, chanted their nighttime antiphon, *ribbit, ribbit, ribbiting,* back and forth to one another, low and comforting. For the moment, everything seemed to be where it was meant to be, doing what it was meant to be doing.

Everything, that is, except John Bunyan and me.

"What are we doing here?" I whispered.

He nodded and winked. "I thought you would never get around to asking." He gestured toward the shadows east of the willow tree. "Do you see that?"

I squinted into the shadows. "Some sort of boat?"

"You are a scholar, Harry, my man," said he. "A boat it is. And we are going to borrow it."

I swallowed hard. "Borrow it? For what?

"For a jaunt on the river."

"A jaunt in a boat?"

"Yes, on the river."

"At midnight?"

"Why not? Most things are more fun in the dark," he replied.

I took a deep breath. "John, there is something I must tell you," I began. I looked anxiously at the water moving past. It suddenly seemed swifter and, more to the point, deeper than before. "I c-cannot swim."

He thumped me on the back, threw his head back and laughed. "Harry, you can't swim?"

I thought he was mocking me, and I cast about for some excuse.

He laughed again. "Have no fear, my good man," said he. "Neither can I!"

I looked at him in astonishment. I had frequent nightmares about not being able to swim. I have heard tell that most people have one thing they are afraid of, terrified of, more than any other. Drowning. For me, it was drowning.

"Look here, Harry," said he. "One only need fear drowning if one fails to stay in the boat."

"One only need fear death by adder bite," I replied, in what seemed to me a most apt rejoinder, "if one attempts to remove its venom sac whilst it is still very much alive, and with one's bare hands."

He looked blankly at me. "Harry, you bewilder me. There's nothing about adders here, eels and boats, but there's nothing to do with adders."

John then climbed down to where the dark shape of the boat hung on its tether. "Come on! Put your fears to rest."

Fool that I was, I followed. "What are we going to do with the boat?"

"Do?" said he. "There is value in merely messing about in boats, some say. However, I am not amongst them. Do you like eels?"

"Do I what?"

"Do you like eels?"

"As pets?"

"No, no, Harry. For eating."

I shuddered. "Eating? My eating of them or their eating of me?"

He laughed, the moonlight twinkling in his eyes. "And some call you a want-wit, Harry. Never let them do that again."

"But what about eels?"

"We are going to borrow this boat," said he, setting the oars in the rowing pins, "and then we are going to borrow some eels."

"Eels, for what?"

"For us to eat, as I said."

"Borrow, you say?"

"Yes, borrow, all in a manner of speaking."

My toes clutching the muddy bank, I squatted next to the boat, my hands trembling on the gunwale. Why did I do it? Follow this madman? I didn't like boats and the water, and I was certain I would not like eating eels. Yet, here I was, casting off the painter, and lowering myself into a boat, on the water, in the dark, to fetch eels. It was madness, indeed. Perhaps, it occurred to me on the instant, for slavishly following him, I was more the madman than he.

Yet, once again, his confidence overmastered my caution. And into that fateful boat I stepped.

Things began to go wrong almost from the first instant we cast away from the banks and into the main stream of the river. One thing was clear to me, John had never rowed a boat before this; or, if he had, he yet needed a great deal more practice in the skill of boat rowing. As I watched his bungling efforts, I imagined even such as I could do far better than he.

"John, this is madness!" I yelled. "The current has taken us! Make haste! Maneuver this infernal thing back to the shore—or we'll perish!"

He swore viciously for reply. But I could see by the moonlight that he was gnawing on his lower lip in consternation, between oaths, as he labored at the oars.

"P-perhaps, if I give it a go?"

More profanity, punctuated by splashing from his oars. And then it happened, all of a sudden, it happened.

John gave a savage pull on his starboard oar, in an attempt, I can only surmise, to navigate us back to the banks of the river and safety. With a crack, the oar shattered into splinters, its blade disappearing into the oily blackness behind us. At the same instant, the boat caught in an eddy and began spinning. John, attempting to steer with but one oar, rose to his feet, jabbing the oar at the water as if to chastise it.

Now at the mercy of the river's current, we passed suddenly through one circling eddy into yet another, but this one spiraling the opposite direction. Heeling precariously, the boat lurched to port. John's body lurched to starboard. Helpless, I watched as he catapulted over the gunwale, moonlight full on his parchment-hued face, his eyes nearly as wide as the black hole that was his screaming mouth.

Sploosh!

John was in the river. I prayed he had been jesting about not knowing how to swim. Sputtering and gasping for breath, he rose to the surface. One look at him flailing about in the water, and I abandoned all hope in his swimming ability.

I was yet in the boat, a boat with no means of propelling or steering it, the current taking me rapidly away from where John had fallen into the abyss-like waters of the River Great Ouse.

In the moonlight I cast about in the boat for something, anything that might float. Then I saw it. A coil of rope, perhaps there for retrieving eel traps. It didn't matter. I snatched it up.

"John! Lay hold of this rope!" I called, then threw with all my might.

I was not certain if he had heard me over all the coughing and splashing. Then, to my eternal relief, I felt the rope go taut. Arm over arm, I pulled, drawing him closer to the boat. I cannot fully express my relief when I saw his fingers, white and trembling, grip the transom of the rowing boat, and then his slickened hair, next appeared his goggling eyes, after which followed his drenched and pallid face, and trembling blue lips.

"Hold fast!" said I. "I have no means of steering this miserable vessel. But there is a bend in the river just ahead. I shall pray that the current will take us to shore." And I did.

When my feet stepped onto the banks of that river, I felt I had been born again, life anew. I said as much to John. He grunted but remained silent. Later when we broke into a barn and curled up shivering in the hay, next to the warm body of a giant old draft horse, I asked him if he believed God had delivered us.

"God? God, you say?" and then he proceeded to launch into a profane diatribe, which, for fear of peril to my soul, I omit to record on these pages.

I listened in astonishment to the proliferation of his cursing. When he paused for breath, I said, "A simple 'no' would have sufficed."

"No, it was not God. It was you, Harry Wylie, you it was delivered us," said he. "Do you recall our years at Harpur Grammar School?"

I said that I did recall them.

"Founded in 1556 by the Lord Mayor of London himself," he continued, "for the teaching of 'grammar and good manners to the children of the poor'?"

I nodded in the affirmative.

"Well, I learned precious little grammar," said he, "and still less of good manners. But I did pick up a verse or two from the Geneva Bible the schoolmaster made us read. Did you know, Harry, that I have taken up a life verse from the pages of Holy Writ? Did you know it?"

I said I did not and wondered that he of all people would have done so. "But I very much would like to hear of it."

"Steady yourself, Harry, for it is a deep one," he warned. "'Depart from me for I do not desire the knowledge of thy ways.' Now, there, Harry, there's a verse to live by, says I."

6

Vulgar Rogue

He thought his life verse a great jest, and laughed so hard at his own joke, that the horse, comforting us free of charge with his great warm flanks, had had enough, and rose onto his massive hooves and hairy fetlocks and made to kick us out of his stall.

Madman, indeed. Here, we had only just been delivered of drowning in the River Great Ouse—not that it mattered which watercourse one drowned in; I supposed drowning was drowning—yet here were we, mercifully delivered from drowning, and all John Bunyan could do was labor to make a profane jest out of the whole incident. No, madmen do not change. I renewed my resolve to part with him, forthwith, knowing all the while that I had done so in vain a hundred times before.

A libertine who resented restraint of any kind, he was a profane madman; and I was not alone in thinking him so, as I shall momentarily relate. I have never seen a young man with a greater greediness of mind for sin, than my youthful companion—unless it was my own self for the crime of following him in it, and breaking my resolve once again. It was as if he had a seared frame of heart, a conscience benumbed by his own foulness.

I had followed him, as was my intractable wont, into the village on a certain day, when John made to hold court, as it were, in the street before a shop window. He threw down the gauntlet of a challenge to the other lads who had gathered. John the ruffian was ever a lad for gathering folk, myself chief amongst the gathered, as I've said.

"I propose," said he, balanced upon a hitching post, the lads pressing in closer about his feet. "I propose a tournament, a contest of eloquence, of syntactical wit, wherein, he who excels—wins the prize."

"What prize, be that?" shouted a fellow at my elbow, his face upturned with eagerness.

Narrowing his eyes conspiratorially, John opened his mouth wide to reply. On the instant, a cur sulking amongst the rubbish in the street drain lifted his head and gave off a guttural bark.

We gathered reprobates tumbled onto the cobbles holding our bellies with great hilarity, much to John's delight.

"What prize, then?" repeated a fellow, when we had recovered ourselves.

Flourishing as if he were a courtier, John extended his hand toward the emaciated cur. "The prize? This fine specimen of a hunting hound; the very best of bloodlines, has she, as you can so readily see."

More hilarity.

Behind John, looking through the leaded window panes at us, stood a woman, her bare arms akimbo on her fulsome hips.

"The worthy prize," he continued in a declaratory monotone, as if he were a royal herald, "will be extended to the man who can most excel in the fine art of cursing, but not just ordinary street cursing. Anyone can excel at that. This exalted cursing will be rendered in the finest poetic rhyme and meter. Now then, who shall go first?"

I pitied the lad who attempted to beat John in that department.

"The contest," snorted a lad behind me, "is no contest."

"Aye, we already know the winner," agreed another fellow.

John frowned and hung his head in feigned disappointment. He was a consummate entertainer, and we all loved it so, as he well knew.

"But word is," said another, "that you've gone and lost your touch."

"Aye, washed up is he," said another, shaking his head. "'Tis such a pity when that happens to a fellow."

I feared what would follow. John was easy prey to this kind of goading.

What came forth from his lips was profanity harmonized with blasphemy, trochaic-metered cursing the likes of which I had never fully heard expressed before that day. Bits and pieces, of course, but it was as if John had been storing it up, counting out the syllables and rehearsing at night on his straw tick mattress, to unleash the foulest doggerel imaginable.

The reader will forgive me for not, herein, setting out its lines. Seared as John's conscience may have been, I yet had some degree of fear of the judgment of the Almighty and of everlasting perdition, which fear restrains my pen from recording his words that day.

What occurred next, demonstrates for all to see, just how vulgar and low John had fallen. The wench-of-a-woman staring at him through that shop window, propelled herself to the doorway. Though the whole village knew her for a loose and ungodly wretch herself, yet had the fearful rate of the profaneness of John's cursing roused the sensibilities even of such a wanton one as she was.

"I tremble to 'ear what spews forth from thy mouth," she screeched. "I 'ave been in the company of the foulest of creatures, but thou, young fool, art the ungodliest fellow for swearing that ever I 'ave 'eard in all my life."

With a wan waggling of his head, and a spiraling of his hand, John bent low before the woman in his version of a courtly bow. "Thank you, milady."

He intoned the words with all the deference of a duke, much to the riotous amusement of we his fellows.

Her face grew red like beetroot. "Away with thee, rogue. Thou wilt spoil all the youth in the whole town. Thou lot, prodding 'im on so. Keep company with the likes of this uncouth ne'er-do-well, and misery and ruin await!"

John passed it off amongst we, his fellow vulgarians, as a great jest, wearing as a badge of honor being publicly so rebuked by the likes of such a woman as she. Yet did I, who knew him best, sense a sobering in him, as if he longed to be a child again, to put off his swearing ways, to use no more oaths before and after every word he made to speak. For a time, he confirmed my suspicions, and took great pride in the outward reforming of himself. Some marveled at the astonishing alteration that, for a time, came over his speech. I knew it would not last, could not last, because men never change.

Sure enough, his reformation had its limits. He would not allow such self-improvement to alter his indulgent pleasure in his games and pranks, as I shall forthwith relate.

7

Village Ruffian

Ringleader in vice and unrivaled vulgarity, as was John Bunyan, as I suspected, his was only a temporary putting off of his outward trespasses. His inward foulness soon stirred itself and with a vengeance. Though his first attempt at outward self-improvement lasted several weeks, I, for one, was surprised it lasted that long. Soon enough, he was restored to his former schemes and pranks. As one Sabbath-day example will suffice to demonstrate.

From where I knelt in the nave of Elstow Abbey that Sabbath morning, I could just see John Bunyan kneeling, as if in reverence. A lovely shaft of sunlight filtered through the stained glass slanted over him, particles of dust floating in that shaft of light looking as if gold dust had been flung in its beam by an enchantress. That golden beam illuminating the likes of John Bunyan seemed to my mind particularly ill placed, like propping a halo on the horns of a devil in a painting.

But, as I have said, he was a consummate actor, and despite the renewed vulgarity of his ways on the other days of the week, he could, if he so desired, play act the penitent, feigning to bring the heavy burden of his sins to the foot of the cross. And here he was doing it on this Sabbath Day, appearing to kneel so reverently next to his father Thomas, his mother Margaret, his sister of the same name, and his little brother William squirming at his side.

Intractably averse to any degree of confinement, John always scrambled for the aisle seat on the bench. Hence, he had positioned himself at the base of one of the massive stone columns supporting the Norman arches, the column closest to the chancel and the south aisle of the abbey, hard by the entombed remains of a late abbess of Elstow, Elizabeth Harvey, who had the misfortune of dying; she had resorted to doing so in the year of our Lord, 1527.

All of which took my mind back to the ancient days when Abbess Judith, niece of William the Conqueror founded the abbey. After his conquest, her uncle arranged for Norman Judith to be married off to the Anglo-Saxon Lord Waltheof, thereby to subdue and subjugate the conquered—or so he had hoped.

We had been taught in grammar school that such matrimonial strategies, though repeatedly attempted, seldom worked well, either for marital bliss or the hoped-for bliss of securing greater political power. Predictably, it did not work well in poor Judith's case.

When she discovered her husband's plot to lead a rebellion in hopes of throwing off the Norman yoke, like a good niece, she shared the intelligence with her uncle. Waltheof shortly thereafter lost his head, and with it his grand Anglo-Saxon moustache. Perhaps as an act of penance for her spousal betrayal, Judith founded the original abbey in 1078, with lavish endowment from Uncle William, King of England.

Unwilling as he was to be hemmed in, I knew John had parked himself there through no particular affection for the moldering remains of the abbess. There was another motive entirely. It provided him with an inconspicuous escape route in the all-too-likely event that he grew bored with the liturgy. I wondered what circumlocution he had scheming in that ever-pregnant imagination of his that morning. I would soon find out, as would we all.

As our vicar Christopher Hall led us in the liturgy from the pages of the Book of Common Prayer, I attempted to tear my mind away from the sordid history of the abbey and concentrate my feeble attention on the words of prayer before us. Searching for divine assistance in the blackened timbers of the ceiling far above, I made to see with the eyes of my body the unseen world perceived, as Vicar Hall often and faithfully reminded us, only through the eyes of faith. Such supernatural vision never worked very well for me, not in my youth.

Soon enough, my mind was awhirl with the stonemason's craft. How did they manage all those many years ago, before all the modern conveniences of our enlightened day, how did such medieval roughs manage to construct so magnificent a chapel? For chapel it was, chapel to the abbey, one of the grandest in all middle England, endowed as it was by the wealth of the very King of England himself, uncle to the aforementioned Abbess Judith.

Lining the nave and rising far above my head were massive round arches cut from honey-colored stones. They appeared to be like the arches from antiquity, from the days when crimson-kilted Roman legions occupied our beloved Britain, that is, if what I had learned at Harpur Grammar School could be trusted.

Behind me to my left was the font, cut from marble, worn with centuries of dousing three-day-old infants in the waters of baptism three times, "in the name of the Father, and of the Son, and of the Holy Ghost." I had, my own self, managed to survive the chilly rite, as had John and his siblings. How effective it had been in washing away the defilement of my heart was greatly in doubt at the present state of things. And if it was in doubt for my own soul, how much more so for the vilest of blasphemers, John Bunyan himself.

It was when our good vicar called us to fall to our knees and repeat the words of confession, "first in the heart and then upon the lips," that I found myself musing on just what mischief John had concocted for that Sabbath. The prayer was good enough, and, however vast the extent of my theological deficiencies, I knew I had plenty to confess, though not as much as the village lawbreaker himself. Of that I was certain as I repeated the words:

"Almighty and most merciful Father; we have erred, and strayed from thy ways like lost sheep. We have followed too much the devices and desires of our own hearts. We have offended against thy holy laws. We have left undone those things which we ought to have done; and we have done those things which we ought not to have done; and there is no health in us. But thou, O Lord, have mercy upon us, miserable offenders. Spare thou them, O God, who confess their faults. Restore thou them that are penitent; according to thy promises declared unto mankind in Christ Jesus our Lord. And grant, O most merciful Father, for his sake; that we may hereafter live a godly, righteous, and sober life, to the glory of thy Holy Name. Amen."

I never was certain when he did it. Snuck out, that is. One moment he was there. The next he was a specter, gone, disappeared, in the twinkling of an eye, like a thief in the night, he had done it. Was it before we confessed that "We have followed too much the devices and desires of our own hearts," or was it sometime after the bit about "we have done those things which we ought not to have done"? So sly was John Bunyan, I was never sure. But he was vacant, not there, vanished.

Our good vicar Christopher Hall proceeded to exhort the peasant folk of our lowly shire about the evils of Sabbath breaking: the worshiping of games and sport, vain activities such as inordinate bell ringing and the imminently forthcoming maypole dancing, much loved by my fellow prankster John Bunyan. The vicar hastened to explain that none of these activities were, in and of themselves, necessarily evils. Yet, our hearts being deceitful above all things and desperately wicked, these things could become idols, and all the more so when engaged in upon a Sabbath Day when our hearts and minds ought to be drawn all the more heavenward, our affections all the more sanctified unto holy things.

As I say, it was just as our good vicar rounded up on his conclusion, that the bells of the belfry began ringing, calling us to come urgently to the aid of our neighbor whose cottage was engulfed in flames. Mind you, the bells themselves can't speak with such eloquence and clarity, but there are conventions, patterns of the ringers' art, that by those conventions have come to speak as eloquently as the Lord Mayor himself.

Breaking off in the middle of the benediction, the vicar looked this way and that in perplexity. A murmur rose throughout the nave of the abbey, with folks turning and looking at the west entrance in bewilderment.

I knew what was afoot. And I knew who was doing it. I could picture John in my mind's eye, his eyes dancing with glee, a wide grin stretching across his ruddy features, his autumn-red hair lifting and splaying madly above him as he rose and fell with the bell pull. I had seen him at it before, been there with him at it my own self.

The church warden rose stiffly to his feet and marched down the center aisle. "Dashed village ruffian up to 'is old tricks again, is 'e."

8

Tip-Cat on the Green

Later that very same Sabbath afternoon, John rallied a following of lads to play a round of tip-cat at the village green. We assembled about the medieval cross on the northwest corner of the green, a vertical shaft carved in stone, a centuries-old place of gathering whether for selling vegetables or raising an army—or for playing at tip-cat.

John tossed a penny high in the air and let it fall. "Heads, I win, tails you lose," said he. Watching the coin twirling and flashing in the momentary sunlight, I recall musing upon where such a one as he might have come by such riches with which to perform the random formality.

Tip-cat is a merry old game, suitable for children and idlers. We had ceased to be the former, all the while desperately holding on to our status as the latter. Mere game that it was, John approached tip-cat as an exalted calling, as if on a par with being a bishop, and he prided himself on his expertise at it.

Placing the cat, a short stick tapered at either end, into the middle of a wooden hoop on the ground, John held his bat under his arm, hocked spittle into his palms, and rubbed them together. Cocking his bat over his shoulder, John's eyes grew narrow. He took sport and games with the deadly seriousness of a life-or-death struggle with an angry bear at a baiting.

Waggling his bat over his shoulder, and pawing his feet in the grass like a bull, he glanced at his fellows with withering condescension. Bringing his bat down with a woosh, he caught the tapered end of the cat. The short stick helicoptered upward, John readying himself by swishing his bat in a circular pattern in anticipation, his eye never leaving the whirling cat. As the short wooden stick reached the zenith of its flight, John grew still more intense, bat poised.

I had seen John hit the cat nigh on the middle of the village green, a great distance measured in hops by the batter, hops which equated to points and winning. Agile and strong, John usually won these contests. On the rare occasion when he did not, he was keen on the instant for a rematch.

But suddenly something changed. I watched in wonder as John's face grew pale. He stood upright, his hands going limp, his bat falling from his fingers, the cat falling harmlessly to the turf. Face upward, John's eyes were wide and darting at the glowering clouds above. It was not like him to be so easily drawn away from sport.

"What is it, John?" I cried, though feeling sure it was a new ruse, part of the game, a novel stratagem he had concocted to win advantage over his fellows. He often resorted to such in sport and games.

It then occurred to me that John might have seen a bird. He was a great one for the watching of birds, seeing and hearing them where I saw or heard not a thing. But then I heard it, *kikikiki*, hovering over the green above us.

"Harry, did you hear him?" His voice was low and hoarse.

I said I had heard him. "A kestrel, is it?"

He shook his head irritably. "That's a merlin." He added absently, "Shorter tail, broader wings."

I followed his heavenward gaze. Odd it was for him to lose at tip-cat for a merlin sighting, and I was about to say so, but he persisted.

"Did you hear him."

"Well, I did hear him," said I, "because you dropped your bat and pointed him out to me."

He gave me one of his withering looks. "Not the merlin," said he, his face once again upturned at the heavens. "Him!"

I eyed him closely, wondering if his fevered mind had at last succumbed to irretrievable madness. "Him? Did you hear the voice of God, John?"

His mouth now agape, he ran a hand through his disheveled hair, and managed to nod for reply.

If this was play acting, he was laying it on like a master of the craft. "What did he say?"

He swallowed hard. In a gravelly whisper he replied, "He said, 'Will you leave your sins and go to heaven, or have your sins and go to hell?' That's what he said, clear as a bell, he said it."

I studied the flat gray sky above us. "Are you sure?"

He glanced at me as if I was the one who had gone daft. "As sure as I'm alive."

"Well, then?"

He remained silent.

"John, if it was the Almighty," I took his arm and gave it a shake. "If it was—that is, if it *was* God. You must be answering him."

The other lads had gathered around us by this time, looking askance at one another and laughing nervously. Nodding knowingly, one lad drew circles in the air with his index finger around his ear. John had done this sort of charade before, though there seemed something different about it this time. Was it yet another of his pranks? We none of us were certain.

"Which is it, then? Heaven or hell?" It was partly in jest that I said this, hoping thereby to awaken him from the trance he had fallen into.

Slowly, his gaze left the heavens and fixed on me. For a full minute he simply stared at me, bland expression, eyes unblinking.

Then, with a deft flick of his toe, he lifted his bat from where he had dropped it, snatched it up in his hand and gave it a spin. "Who's cat?" He asked it as if nothing had happened, as if there had been no voice. He'd had his turn at tip-cat. Who was up next?

Later that afternoon, as we idled our way along the cart ruts of the narrow road back to Harrowden, he confided in me. "I felt a great burden upon my spirit, Harry, at his words, did I."

"At God's words?"

"No, at the vicar's, in his sermon."

"John, how could the vicar's words trouble you so? I saw you my own self. You had skulked your way out of the church while the rest of us were confessing our miserable offenses, well before he began his exhortation."

"True, but I stood and listened for a time."

"But if it troubled you so," said I, "how is it that you went off and rang the bells in spite of all?"

"I shook the sermon out of my mind," said he, "and my heart returned to its old course." He made a vicious swing of his stick at the hedgerow bordering the highway. "The fire of that sermon went out. *Poof*, just like that, it went out. And glad I was of it. Its trouble was gone from me, and I could resume my sin without control."

"John, you puzzle me. Why are you troubled now, then?"

"When the words came to me from the heavens," he replied, "it was as if I had, with the eyes of my understanding, seen the Lord Jesus looking down at me. Harry, he was most displeased, was he." He shuddered before resuming his words. "And he was severely threatening some grievous punishment for my great and grievous sins."

As he explained these things to me, I observed him responding to his own words, his eyes wide and staring for a time, but gradually resuming that mischievous sparkling I had so often observed in him before.

"But, then," he continued, his voice returning to his more usual tone, "as I mused on what a great and grievous sinner I have been, it occurred to me that the Almighty might just have given up on me, that it was now too late for the likes of me, that he would not forgive or pardon my manifold transgressions."

I attempted to interject, to say that I believed I had heard the vicar say something to the contrary, but he held up his hand for silence.

"My heart sinking into despair," he continued, his voice hushed with wonder, as if he had fallen under the mesmerizing spell of his own narrative, "I reasoned that if I was miserable but it was far too late for me to repent—" He broke off for dramatic effect. "Well, then," said he with a wink, "I might as well be damned for many sins as be damned for but few!"

9

Dancing

I had this vague but terrifying notion in my mind that every time John Bunyan passed through a sobering moment, a moment where he felt some degree of the weight of his own wickedness, however fleetingly; I had it in my mind that it might just be having an accumulative effect on his condemnation. Each successive contemplative episode he passed over, after which returning once again to his wickedness, might not it be a heaping up of greater wrath at the hand of the Almighty on the judgment day?

I say, I had this in my mind—and more than once I lay awake in a cold sweat about it—but if such a notion ever came to the mind of John Bunyan, it did not act as a deterrent in any measurable degree. Far from it. He plunged into successive episodes of villainy with the exuberance of a snowball tumbling faster and ever larger down a steep hill to destruction and ruin, the more accelerated the plummeting the more raucous his glee at the fall, so it seemed.

New depths of that plummeting I observed on the first of May, 1644, the village green alive with color, laughter, and merriment. The annual market fair had come to the village, with merchants and their wares from all over Europe gathered for buying and selling, entertaining and eating, drinking and dancing. No one looked forward to the ancient celebration of springtime and the maypole more than John Bunyan.

But on that May Day, John's father Thomas, recovering from a cold in the head, required his son to ply the family trade in his stead for the hundreds gathered.

I caught sight of John, shuffling along Church End, the burden of the family anvil balanced on his right shoulder, a coarse sac slung over his left. I knew its weighty contents: sheets of tin, rivets, solder, punches, and an assortment of hammers. Puffing, he halted at the west end of the timbered Moot Hall, scanning the turf thereabouts with a critical eye.

The Bunyan anvil, mind you, was unlike a blacksmith's anvil in shape. A tinker's anvil, I had been told, had to be portable, easily carried from one cottage to the next. The Bunyan anvil was more like a nail, a great iron nail, nearly the length of a man's leg, but heavier. I had once attempted to hoist the thing onto my shoulder, an effort that made me look heavenward with gratitude that my father was a mere tenant farmer.

With a grunt, John heaved the anvil off his shoulder. It was carefully aimed. Using the prodigious weight of the anvil itself, he let it bury its pointed end into the turf, leaving the round pounding surface at the ready.

John greeted me and then began whistling as he arranged the tools and materials of his trade. Compared to the exotic displays being erected about the green, booths and pavilions from faraway places, merchants displaying their exotic wares from Italy, France, Spain, Germany, John's was a wholly unimpressive exhibit. But I knew from past experience, he had a succession of schemes for making up deficiencies.

"Harry, my man," said he, "would you be so kind as to fetch me a hot coal from that cooking fire just there?" He nodded with his head toward an Italian merchant a few yards away. An iron pot hung from a tripod over the coals, steam and aromatic vapors rising above it. I closed my eyes and drew in breath through my twitching nostrils. I do not exaggerate to say, that from within that cooking pot rose the most heavenly of aromas—oregano, tomatoes, pesto, basil, beef broth—I could not wholly differentiate the divine medley of flavors that therein mingled, simmering to our torment.

Once John had his fire hot and glowing, he strapped on his one-legged stool. "Pots to mend," he called to passersby, "knives to grind—any work for the tinker?" It was a comical sight, that single leg wagging behind him like a rigid tail on a dog walking on its hind legs.

"Pots to mend, knives to grind—any work for the tinker?"

Squatting, he added his own two legs to make a three-legged sitting place while he worked, he began tapping on the anvil. But not just any tapping. I watched in wonder as John, his ears cocked, weighed his various hammers in his hands, then laid them out onto his knees. He snatched different ones up as he played his version of a symphony on the anvil, accompanied by his whistling. He was ever one for music, music and poetry, was he.

Ever the gatherer, John's antics that morning brought folks to watch and listen, and more than a few folks with pots that needed mending. To our gastronomical delight, the Italian merchant hard by had a tin pot for steaming vegetables that had developed a fracture as long as a man's hand. Heating solder over the coals, in short order, John welded the crack until he had the pot as serviceable as new. In exchange, John and I dined on a mouthwatering Italian soup.

Business lagged after luncheon, but John was not to be put off, and busied himself with a project, cutting sheets of tin, braising joints, flaring rivets, and always tap-tapping with his hammers.

"What is it to be, John?"

He eyed me from the underbrush of eyebrows. "Watch and see."

As the creation took shape, more folks gathered to watch the young tinker at his craft.

"Is it—?" I began, but he halted me by holding up an open palm.

"Not yet," said he. "Harry, I need you to gather horse hairs for me."

"Horse hairs?"

"Indeed, from a horse," said he. "Preferably from the tail of the beast, long and straight ones."

"How many horse hairs?"

"I'll be needing only four," said he, "but bring me more so I can choose just the right ones."

I returned sometime later, rubbing my shins. While I had been helping myself to a horse's hairs, the beast had given me a swift kick. John had been busy. More than two dozen onlookers watched as he put the finishing touches on his creation.

"A fiddle?" said I. "Aren't they ordinarily made of wood not tin?"

He gave me a withering look. "Harry, I know nothing of this word 'ordinarily' that you use. Anyone can make a violin from wood, as the world-wide inventory of violins will attest. Only a master tinker can craft one from tin."

Master conniver that he was, I knew no one who could so make the ridiculous seem not only probable but the only reasonable way of it.

After fitting the horsehairs in place, John rose to his feet and proceeded to entertain the crowd—now more than three dozen, and pressing in close—by playing his tin violin, his one-legged stool wagging behind as he swayed to his own melody. I feared he might accompany himself by breaking into the singing of his own spontaneous, profane poetry.

Suddenly, a merry fanfare of drums, cornetto, viols, and sackbuts drowned out John's tin fiddle playing. Stout men from the village paraded behind the musicians carrying a fresh-cut ash pole, long, wide ribbons of crimson, yellow, and blue affixed to its top. The music halted as the men in silent ceremony erected the pole in the center of the green. The music resumed.

Staring as if in a stupor of longing at the sight, John's tin fiddle fell from his hands.

"Harry, watch my things," said he, making to follow the procession to the pole.

"John! Your stool," I called after him, pointing at his posterior. I doubted that it would bother him overmuch, but the thought of him prancing about around the maypole with his one-legged stool pointing the other way, would have been outlandish to observe, and I knew he would be a laughingstock.

Hastily, he unbuckled his one-legged stool, and nearly ran to the pole.

"Another thing is my dancing," John had once admitted to me during one of his remorseful moments. He knew why the vicar and other Puritan clergyman wanted to be done with such dancing about the pole on the first of May. John Bunyan didn't plunge into his wickedness without knowledge. He was ever the careful scholar of his naughtiness. "You know its origins, don't you, Harry?" I had assured him I did not. I thought it all merely an innocent springtime activity, and had said so.

Tut-tutting my naiveté, John had gone on to illuminate my darkness. "Maypole dancing is ancient, stretching back as far as the painted Celts, centuries long past." He had explained this as if he had been there. "It was a pagan fertility festival called Beltane. Harry, you understand the word 'fertility,' do you not?"

I had pretended to understand it fully, though I doubt that he believed me.

"Beltane was the spring festival of the Celtic fertility cult," he began, intoning as he imagined a lecturer at the university in nearby Cambridgeshire would speak. "The pole was understood to be a phallic symbol, erected in the midst of the village green. The male and female dancers would take hold of the colorful ribbons and braided branches, dancing in and out, whirling around the pole, sensuously entwining in and around and through one another as they danced. As a pagan religious rite, the dancing was symbolic of the fertility that comes from men and women entwining themselves in the act of procreation. The dancing, thus, becoming a liturgical offering to the pagan gods in hopes that the gods will bring fertility to their crops, to their cattle, and to their cradles."

He had paused here, presumably to give me opportunity to express wonder at his elocution.

I had swallowed hard at his words. "If what you say is true, it's little wonder the Puritans want to be done with such dancing."

I recollected this conversation as I watched John take hold of a bright crimson ribbon and begin cavorting about the pole. Most of the dancers had come prepared, dressed in white gowns or shirts and trousers, but John wore his usual laboring clothing—his only clothing—the sheep-butt, brown homespun of the peasant class. Yet, for all that, he footed it well.

Looking back on May of 1644, with all of its festivities and celebration, unbeknownst to us at the time, soon to be turned to woe and mourning, I wondered at what the vicar called "the mystery of the providence of God." How rapidly life could go from joy to sorrow, from normality to upheaval, from plenty to poverty, from health and strength to weakness and death—I was about to experience all this. As was John Bunyan.

10

War and Influenza

I once observed that there were but few calamities, public hangings, and other exciting things going on in mundane middle England. That was about to change.

Word was, that in faraway London, King Charles I was not getting along so well with Parliament. We gathered most of our news from hearsay at The Jetty, the covered staging place for the coach from London to Bedford, where the latest news was exchanged at The White Lion, the adjoining coaching inn.

We learned that the Puritan and Protestant Parliament had become increasingly suspicious of the king's wife, French Roman Catholic Henrietta Maria. There had been a long tug-of-war going on between the members of Parliament who felt that the king was taking far more of the share of power than the Magna Carta and a limited monarchy allowed.

The king, on the other hand, believed that he ruled by divine right, and that neither the people, their representatives, any human court, nor parliament had any authority over his rule and will—the long history of a limited monarchy in England notwithstanding. His sentiments about his absolute rule were much noised abroad: "It is not for having share in government, sirs; that is nothing pertaining to the people. A subject and a sovereign are clear different things." Royalists unflinchingly agreed. Puritan Parliamentarians did not, and a great deal of flinching would result.

Eventually, Charles I, greedy for still more power, with a bold stroke of his bejeweled scepter, dissolved Parliament—three times, he did it. By 1642, the tug-of-war erupted into a full-blown civil war. Armies were raised throughout the shires of England, some to support the king, while many others to stand with Parliament and the Puritan cause.

Mind you, John and I were but lads of fourteen years when first this much-longed-for calamity fell upon England. Too young to enlist and fight, we were much unaffected by the conflict, to John's great disappointment, if not to mine.

Meanwhile, without our knowing of it, another calamity was poised to fall upon us—invisible, silent, and sinister—it was most particularly, to fall upon John Bunyan and his family.

It began when dozens of people in Elstow and Bedford fell suddenly under a pestilent ague, the body inflamed, aches and pains throughout every limb, a raspy throat, and an uncontrollable coughing. But for many the symptoms grew worse: severe fatigue, a loosening of the stools, thundering congestion of the head. Within a fortnight, the influenza grew still worse. The constricting of the nose and throat became so severe that the ability to breathe in and out ceased with a whimper. Death came hard on the heels.

All this fell upon the Bunyan hovel in June of 1644. Within a few weeks, under the severities of the pestilence, John's mother and sister expired. Under body-shaped mounds of fresh earth, they were laid to rest with dozens more in the church yard of the abbey.

Without a word to his son, John's father remarried, taking to himself his third wife. Only a few short weeks had passed since the death of his second wife, John's mother.

John's grief turned to anger at his father for his over-hasty remarriage. And he told him of his anger.

"What was I to do?" said his father, though he said it after the marriage had already been solemnized by the vicar. "I must work at my calling, and I get precious little help from you, John—you wasted your time and my materials on a tin violin? If I don't repair the pots and pans of the rich and the poor, there's nothing for us on the table, no food, no drink. How am I to work at my calling and care for the house and little William? It's not possible without a woman on hand. A poor tinker, such as I, can ill afford to hire a serving woman. So, another wife it must be, and there's an end of it."

I secretly hoped that in his distress, John would come to a more tender frame of mind and leave off his ambition to be damned for many sins as for few. But deep down I knew it was a vain hope indeed. Madmen do not change.

For weeks John fumed and railed, cursed and swore at the unmerciful heavens above him. Until one day he read a poster nailed to the door of The White Lion calling for enlistments in the army. His entire countenance was transformed on the instant.

Inwardly, I groaned. By the look in his eye, I knew that his imagination was ignited at the prospect. "You and me, Harry," said he, leaping onto the coach block at The Jetty, "'If we are marked to die, we are enough to do our country loss, but if to live, the fewer men, the greater share of honor.' Think on it, Harry. Honor and glory in the war—it's ours for the taking."

I laughed nervously at him, hoping it was another one of his jests. "I've never been much for seeking honor."

"Oh, but Harry, stick with me," said he. "'If it be a sin to covet honor, I am the most offending soul alive!'"

So, it was that John set off for the garrison in Newport Pagnell thirteen weary miles away to the west to enlist himself in the Parliamentary Army, there to give himself, body and soul, to the treasonous activity of fighting against the Crown. And I, fool that I was, trotted trembling at his heels.

I shall never forget my terror when it was finally our turn to stand before the table-side of the enlisting officer, his quill poised over his inkhorn.

"Set down my name, sir!" John said the words as if he were the Earl of Essex himself, eager for battle, sword drawn, stout and ready for deadly force; I could just imagine him cutting and hacking his way through the enemy, falling on all comers, fearlessly pressing forward into the breach.

But, so baleful-eyed and speechless was I when it was my turn at the enlisting table, John Bunyan had to give off my name for me. "Harry Wylie, is he, sir. Valiant and true, is he, sir."

The enlisting officer hesitated, frowning at the scrawny lad shivering before him. "We shall see about that," said he. "How do ye spell 'Wylie'?" he growled. "Never mind. It doesn't matter," he added, scribbling with his quill.

Enlisting was only the beginning of my terrors. For the next three years, most days I felt on the brink of swooning. War was a dangerous business, as I shall relate, and I daily berated myself for following him into it. But to turn back now meant desertion, and desertion for a soldier, I was to learn, meant hanging by the neck until dead.

We were barely of an age to enlist and be much good at the fighting. But John had the advantage on me. His frame was broad and sturdy, and he stood a head taller than most young men his age—our age, which was but sixteen years each.

What we experienced in the army left scars on us both. John was loath to speak or write about what we saw and what we did as soldiers in the English Civil War. From his reticence to divulge more details of our activities in the war, some have wrongly concluded that we merely polished boots and fed horses, nothing more, no real fighting. But those who conclude thus, know little of the effects of war, of fighting, of killing, of daily living under the fear of one's own dying, on the men so engaged, as were we.

The calamity we had longed for had come upon us. And I frequently rued the day of those foolish, boyhood longings.

After banning maypole dancing in 1644, as "a heathenish vanity, generally abused to superstition and wickedness," Lieutenant-General Oliver Cromwell devised improved military measures to create a New Model Army, as it was called, in the wheels of which army we, John and I, were to be blood-red-coated cogs.

11

Training for War

R oundheads we both are now," said John our first evening in the army together.

The Parliamentary garrison at Newport Pagnell to which we were attached had no fine coaching inn accommodations for the likes of John and me. Our billet was a stained canvas tent, hastily erected, the last tent in the seemingly endless rows of tents lined up on a field hard by the convergence of the River Great Ouse and the River Lovat. We were not alone.

We had been issued a red coat, and boots for marching in, both pieces of equipment appearing to have been worn and patched after being used by others. With great effort, I forced my mind not to dwell over-much on why it was these men no longer needed boots and coat.

Next, we were given our first daily ration of a single pound of round biscuit and one pound of cheese; we would discover that most days were cheese days, but occasionally we were given a pound of salt beef or pork instead of the cheese. We were expected to supply our own cutlery and bowl or trencher. Poor lads that we were, neither of us owned such luxuries. We ate with our hands.

"Roundhead." I mused on the word while attempting to chew on a biscuit that felt like petrified wood between my teeth. "It doesn't sound overly complimentary."

John agreed. "But I'd far rather be a Roundhead than a Cavalier, a foreigner with French or Spanish affiliations, like King Charles has, hence the name. But I prefer the better name for our army."

"What better name is that?"

"'Ironsides,' we're called," said he.

"A fitting name for these biscuits," I observed, my jaw beginning to ache.

"We've earned the name Ironsides, have we," continued John as if it was his very own personal achievement, "because of our fortitude."

John could be like that, all grandiose in speech and manner. I frowned at the cheese. "Is your cheese green with mold like mine?" I tried breaking my hunk into pieces and separating out the green bits.

"It's supposed to be that way," said John, "or at least it helps to tell yourself that. Eat it with a biscuit."

"An iron biscuit, you mean," I murmured.

Red coat, boots, and food ration, such as it was, were not the only items we were given that first day. After swearing loyalty to the Parliamentary cause, a logistics officer had issued each man a copy of The Soldier's Pocket Bible. It was a small pamphlet, far from the whole Bible, easily to be slipped into the inner pocket of our waistcoat nearest the heart. Its sixteen pages contained 150 passages about soldiering and war from the sacred pages of the Geneva Bible. I expected John Bunyan to scorn the booklet, but was surprised at the attention he gave to the pamphlet Bible for soldiers.

"'The Soldier's Pocket Bible,'" read John, using his rucksack under his head for a pillow, his ankles crossed. "'Containing the Most (if Not All) Of Those Places Contained in Holy Scripture, Which Do Show the Qualifications of His Inner Man, That Is a Fit Soldier to Fight the Lord's Battles, Both Before the Fight, in the Fight, and After the Fight,' so it says right on the front cover."

I listened while hammering a biscuit into crumbs with a rock. I expected him to snort and scoff with oaths; but, to my surprise, he didn't do it.

"Harry, had you heard?" he continued, looking at me over the top of his copy of the pamphlet Bible. "Since Oliver Cromwell issued The Soldier's Pocket Bible in 1643, just last year, the armies of Parliament have not lost a single battle. Had you heard?"

I told him I had not heard, and wondered aloud how he had heard such superstitious twaddle.

"I pay close heed to intelligence like that," he replied, tapping his head with an index finger. "I, for one, plan to keep my copy close to my heart." He said this, stuffing his copy into an inner pocket, and patting it reverently.

"What, as a talisman?" I wasn't truly surprised at his words. "You think that by the mere carrying of a portion of the Bible in your pocket your safety in battle is assured? Is that your thinking?"

He shrugged. "It can't hurt."

"If there's good to be found in it," said I, opening my copy, "I'm thinking it'll come from reading therein." And so, I opened my copy and made to read aloud to us both.

"'When thou goest out with the host against thine enemies, keep thee then from all wickedness.'" I paused, eyeing John over the pages.

His eyes half closed like the statue of a saint, he nodded with pious-seeming approval at the words. Then, I saw the light of his imagination flicker. He sat up and turned to a blank page at the end of his pocket Bible, and began scribbling with a piece of charcoal. After a few minutes, he cleared his throat and read aloud.

"Who would true valor see." John said the words deliberately while counting out the meter on his fingers, stopping occasionally to scratch a word out and write another in its place.

"Let him come hither.
One here will constant be
Come wind, come weather.
There's no discouragement
Shall make him once relent
His first avowed intent
To be a soldier."

He looked up at me with that wide grin that so often stretched across his ruddy face.

81

"What do you think?" he asked. "As needed, I can alter the final word to suit the occasion: hero, lieutenant-general, lord-general—"

I broke in on his fantasy. "—ruffian, scoundrel, sinner, madman. Yes, it is a most pliable verse, indeed."

He hurled a biscuit my direction, I dodging it as if it were a stone or an iron hammer.

I have recorded that our stained canvas tent was one of a multitude of tents stretching row-upon-row across the fields hard by the convergence of the two rivers. Hence, we were never alone in our billet.

And with thousands of men encamped in close proximity, I learned that it is not possible to do so without endless noise. I was on the brink of a life of the same. So seldom was there any silence in our lives while in the army that for the next thirty-two months of our lives my ears were plagued with an undulation of ringing sounds.

Though I would soon enough discover that noise in a battle was far worse, that first night of our encampment at Newport Pagnell rang with a cacophony of human sounds filling the air: shouting and laughter, the clanking of pots and pans, the timpani of drums, the hammering of the blacksmith, the snorting and neighing of horses, the moaning of the wounded, digging sounds with spades, a snatch of the coarse strains of bawdy singing, and the exalted refrains of psalm singing. There was far more of the latter than the former, we were to learn, in the Parliamentary Army into which we had enlisted ourselves.

In the midst of all these new sounds assaulting our ears, John and I made a most extraordinary acquaintance that very first night, one that would prove to be of the greatest consequence for John Bunyan, as I shall hereafter relate.

All the while that evening, we had been adding to the noise by talking about hard biscuits, moldy cheese, the Bible, and John making up more of his poetry. Our tent was pitched only a boot-width from the next tent, but we had paid no heed to the taciturn, middle-aged man sitting in front of the one hard by ours. It was impossible for him not to have heard every word we had spoken— impossible unless from the thundering of cannon fire he had entirely lost all sense of hearing.

After reading out his pliable verse, John sat up and turned toward the silent man, as if seeing him for the first time. "My name is John Bunyan, good sir, and this is Harry Wylie. We are new here, new recruits, sir."

The man nodded, slowly setting down a pewter mug. "Worthington, Ezra Worthington," said he, his voice low and raspy.

Ezra Worthington was a giant of a man. He dwarfed the folding camp stool on which he sat, elbows on his knees, leaning toward a small coal fire, his hands clasped together into a calloused, double-fisted mound. He wore a battered leather buff coat and bucket-top boots, the flame from his fire shimmering on the leather and sparkling in his pale gray eyes. And with those eyes he sat staring at us, steady and penetrating.

I swallowed. My first impression of Worthington, when once I looked more closely, was relief that he was on our side and not on the side of our enemy. There was strength in the mysterious man. Not just in his broad chest and powerful shoulders and arms, but something more, something emanating from within him, an immoveable inner posture that I could not wholly explain or understand.

By the scars on his hands and one running gash-like alongside his throat and neck, he was clearly not a new recruit. Everything about him suggested the man was a rock of military experience. I mused on the story that his scars could tell. Novice to battle that I was, it was impossible for me to imagine the bloody campaigns in which he had engaged.

All this while, he said not a word, only sat appraising us with his pale gray eyes. I wondered at the mystery of God's providence placing us for neighbor by such a man as he. And then I heard John draw in breath to speak. I feared what words might emit from his mouth.

"Sir, you've likely as not deduced this already," said John, his voice more sober than I believe I had ever heard him. "We, Harry and me, know absolutely nothing about soldiering."

I nodded in agreement.

"Do you have words of wisdom," continued John, "for novices such as we?"

Worthington, who appeared to be older than either of our fathers back in Harrowden, took so long replying, I feared he had concluded we were a hopeless cause as soldiers. There was no wisdom that could deliver the likes of us.

"Obey orders," said he in his low guttural voice, "and hope in God."

John fidgeted at my side, and I feared he was about to give himself up for the blasphemer that I knew him to be. "I was hoping, sir," said John, "that you could help us become soldiers, good soldiers, maybe, someday, even valiant soldiers."

Another long pause. "I have done," said he. "Obey orders, and hope in God."

We jolted awake next morning to the shrill call of trumpets and the thundering of drums. Our life in the army had begun. To our great surprise, we were assigned to a training officer, none other than our nearest neighbor in the vast field of tents, Sergeant Ezra Worthington.

In the midst of the rigors of our military training, we soon discovered that Sergeant Worthington, whatever he might have lacked in the finer leadership qualities needed for higher ranking officers, the man more than made up for in his keen sense of the art of warfare. I came to believe this was because the man had an almost uncanny ability to appraise and then equip other men, both in body and in mind, and, we were to learn, in their hearts.

Under his watchful eye, we learned to march, carry a flintlock musket, prime, load, and fire our muskets; form up in ranks, form a line for giving volley fire—and how to remain undaunted in the receiving of the same from the enemy. And we learned, to my horror, how to wield our muskets as clubs, should it come to it, in hand-to-hand combat. And still more marching, always marching.

Our affection for Worthington grew hourly. He was not a yelling sergeant; indeed, it was rumored, though he never wasted words telling of it, that his wound in the throat was received while fighting on the Continent in defense of German Protestants against imperial Spanish tyrants, a wound that seriously damaged his vocal chords, and so was he wholly incapable of yelling at us in our training. The more we came to know the man, however, I came to the settled conclusion that with or without an ability to yell, he never would have done so. He had far better methods.

Our reverence for our good sergeant grew hourly. He was determined to make soldiers out of us, and he knew exactly what skills we needed to acquire if we were to survive battle against the enemy. And he knew the best methods for our acquiring of those skills.

At the end of each day, John and I were so exhausted, that after consuming our biscuits and cheese, and washing it down with small beer, we collapsed into our tent to sleep like dead men.

After a fortnight of hard training, just before drifting off bone weary to our sleep, I recall a conversation we had about our sergeant.

"Marching, drilling, digging, more marching," murmured John, his hands clasped behind his head, he staring at the stained canvas above us, moonlight filtering dimly through the tent. "Our Sergeant Worthington is a hard-driving taskmaster, is he."

I agreed. "But he's more than that. Man of few words that he is, I believe he treats us more like—" I broke off searching for the right word.

"—Like we're his kin?"

I turned, leaning on my elbow. "That's it." I recalled Sergeant Worthington's unremitting toughness with us, yet was it seasoned with a gruff tenderness, and his many acts of kindness: sharing extra rations with us, fitting us out with leather jerkins, sturdy leather gloves, and bucket-top boots more suited to the shape of our feet for marching in. "It's as if he treats us," I hesitated, "like we're his sons."

John grunted in agreement. I felt too weary for more words, and rolled onto my side. Just as I was drifting off, his words jolted me back to wakefulness.

"Harry, have you noticed it?" said he.

"Noticed what?"

"The shape of it."

I opened one eye and looked his way in the dim light.

"The stain on our tent," said he. "It's in the shape of a man, a body—see, there's its trunk, its legs, its head. I'm thinking this swathe of canvas had another use before it became our tent."

On that cheery note, my weariness was overtaken by anxiety. John rolled on his side and was soon fast asleep. Meanwhile, my mind was awhirl with apprehension. What lay ahead for us in the war? Our first battle, when would it be? Were we ready? Would we, John and me, would we survive it, the battle, the war?

I must have drifted off to sleep, because next thing I knew my anxious thoughts were interrupted by the penetrating cadence of the trumpet calling us to wake and ready ourselves for another day of training.

"Up you go, Harry," said John, throwing off his field blanket and stretching like a tomcat after a night prowl.

I groaned. It was time to do it again. When would it end? Another fortnight, a month, six months, a year? I shuddered. We were always training, always marching, always priming, loading, and firing, always parrying and sparring with our muskets, and for what? For that first day when it would not be training anymore. We'd be facing off with the enemy, real men hell-bent on our destruction, in a real battle.

12

Keep Your Powder Dry

June 14, 1645, one hour past midnight, all the world as black as Hades. I shivered. Or was it trembling? Though similar in effect, there is a different cause to each, as I had come to know so well.

It was unseasonably chilly that early morning, and a clammy fog hung in the air, forming into beads of moisture on my helm. Yes, helm. Sergeant Worthington, ever looking out for our safety and equipping, had issued lobster helmets to John and me. From its battered scars and dents, I believed mine had been used by another, as had John's. My eyes were wide as I attempted to view the dark and clammy world through the visor grid of my helm that morning.

The night air was scented with gun powder and the pinching aroma of fear-induced sweat. Pungent as the sweat of 3,000 infantry men-at-arms is, I wondered if the enemy would smell us before they heard us. I was momentarily comforted with the thought that the Royalist troops, outnumbered by our army and poorly led, were no doubt emitting their own sweaty stench.

I had heard that previous to the command of Lieutenant-General Oliver Cromwell and his New Model Army, soldiers did not go on night marches in English warfare. All that had changed. It was very much a night march on which we were engaged in the early morning hours of June 14, 1645.

And an uphill march it was. I felt my heart in my throat with every tread. Here I was at the booted heels of John Bunyan, once again, and just ahead of him in our column was our Sergeant Ezra Worthington. Stretching out in single-file, behind and before us, marched 3,000 soldiers of foot. We dutifully followed as our commander General Philip Skippon led our infantry division up a winding track to the high ground above where Prince Rupert of the Rhine reportedly had set up his defenses.

General Skippon had issued the command at midnight when we set out, a command that had successively filtered itself down through the chain of command. We were to march in total silence, never speaking a word aloud. "Not so much as a sneeze, lads," cautioned our sergeant as he related the command in a gravelly whisper in our ears.

So, we had set out an hour ago, every man of our 3,000 carrying a matchlock musket as we wound our way up that track to the high ground. The matchlock musket, the very latest firearm weapon of the age, required each man of us to ignite our match, a short piece of rope that had been boiled in saltpeter, and to keep it aglow by steady puffs of oxygen from our lungs. If any of us allowed our match to fizzle out, just when it was time to thrust the match into the priming powder in the pan, present and give fire, nothing would happen. There could be no firing of the weapon without a lit match. No firing of the weapon meant we were easy prey for our enemy.

So it was that we had been trained in a steady pattern of marching three steps and as we took the fourth, blowing gently on our match so as to be at the ready for firing at short notice.

Even on the brink of a bloody battle, I was to learn, there can be moments of sublime beauty. Gazing up into the darkness through the iron grid of my visor, I watched in wonder as our line snaked its way up the track toward the high ground. Our matches all aglow, we became a long curving line, each man a flickering speck of light, refracted and flaring out through the water particles of the fog. Unseen by the enemy on the other side, we had become like a giant glow worm slithering up that hill.

I was momentarily both awed and calmed by the sight, and in that frame of mind I began recalling what I had heard the night before.

Only hours ago, we had heard a sermon by John Gibbs, a young Puritan preacher, chaplain to our company. "'Be valiant and fight the Lord's battles. Be strong, and let us be valiant for our people, and for the cause of our God, and let the Lord do what is good in his eyes.'"

Though Mr. Gibbs was but two years our senior in age, John and I had become much affected by the sermons of the man, by his words, yes, but also by his deeds, his unadorned goodness. Much affected, I say, though I ever feared that John's outward semblance of piety, was like his boots, as easily taken off as put on.

And then, after Gibbs' sermon, General Philip Skippon commander of our infantry, gave us our orders and mustering places for the night march. After which our commander led us in the singing of a Psalm. Words fail me to describe the sound. We were the voices of 3,000 soldiers of foot facing the most important engagement of the entire war, and some of us would die that next day. And so, we sang as if our very lives depended upon that singing, and there was an infectious camaraderie that resulted, wherein we encouraged one another, our voices swelling, growing louder, almost shouting:

The Lord of hosts is with us,
The God of Jacob is our Refuge!

I sincerely hoped the words of Psalm 46 were true for us that June 14, 1645. Amidst these sober recollections, I plodded upward, always in the footsteps of my companion John Bunyan, carrying myself in my own boots, so I feared, to my doom.

In the numb hours of that march, I both longed for the day and dreaded it more than words can express. As I have learned, my longing or dreading had no effect on the irrepressible turning of heavenly bodies. It happened so gradually that it was difficult to discern when the darkness ended, and the cold, blue-gray light of dawn revealed to my sight the wispy tentacles of fog clinging to the low ground stretching out below us.

After achieving the high ground in our long march, there no longer remained a need for concealment from our enemy. Now was the time for making noise. General Skippon's field musicians, trumpeters and drummers, played no small role in preparing us for battle that morning. Forming in ranks, their rope-tension drums slung over their shoulders, drummers began their ruffles, exhilarating to our side but ominous and foreboding to our enemies—or so I hoped. Along with the trumpeters, our drummers conveyed orders to our whole regiment with clarity and precision. Without the thundering of the drums and the flourishing of the trumpets, penetrating through and above the cacophony created by the movement of thousands of men of foot, and equal numbers of cavalry, none of us would have known where to form in ranks, what to do next, and when to do it.

We were accustomed to singing Psalms in strict versification, but, General Skippon and many of his infantry soldiers alongside whom we fought in the Parliamentary Foot, had fought in the German Protestant wars of religion against the multinational mercenary forces of the Spanish-Catholic, Holy Roman Empire.

German Protestants went into battle singing their battle hymn *Ein Feste Berg*, its lyric drawn from Psalm 46. Skippon had been so taken with the melody and the words of the hymn written and composed by the Reformer Martin Luther in the last century, that he often led his men in singing Luther's version thereof, and John and me with them, as we did that morning.

> A mighty fortress is our God,
> A bulwark never failing;
> Our helper he, amid the flood
> Of mortal ills prevailing:
> For still our ancient foe
> Doth seek to work us woe;
> His craft and power are great,
> And, armed with cruel hate,
> On earth is not his equal.

John sang loud and lustily at my side. From the first time we sang, John was much taken with its cadences and melody, if not its theology. I often heard him humming the tune to himself whilst going about our duties around the garrison. Singing it that morning at Naseby, eyeing through the fog King Charles' and Prince Rupert's Royalist army of 9,000 desperate men, lodged a lump in my throat that felt like I had swallowed an iron biscuit whole, with no effort at chewing.

After the final strain of *Ein Feste Berg* fell from our lips, General Skippon addressed our infantry, his voice booming over the rumbling cartwheels of our cannons, and the thundering of hooves. "Trust in God," said he, "but mind you, keep your powder dry." Skippon hastened to give credit for this admonition to Lord Acton who had said the same to his soldiers in another battle.

94

Shoulder-to-shoulder we the Parliamentary Soldiers of Foot, readied our muskets and awaited orders, blowing on our matches, waiting at the ready, my innards churning like Elstow Water after a spring tempest.

13

Battle of Naseby

With waiting comes worry, so I learned. We waited and I worried, gnawing the inside of my cheek with apprehension as both armies maneuvered for strategic advantage on the ridges and hills alongside the town of Naseby.

It was rumored that the tide of the war had shifted decidedly against the Royalist cause. Perhaps in his anxiety over the fact, Prince Rupert had a lapse in judgment. He inexplicably abandoned a superior defensive position and ordered his force to march toward our side and take up a position on Dust Hill, a barren ridge, precarious and indefensible.

I could only imagine his worry as he surveyed our army, 14,000 combined men of foot and cavalry. Formed in ranks alongside Skippon's infantry, where I trembled in my boots, stood the New Model Soldiers of Foot under Lord-General Thomas Fairfax. Protecting our left flank was General Henry Ireton's cavalry, and, on our right, the New Model cavalry under the command of Lieutenant-General Oliver Cromwell himself.

And still we waited—I growing more wide-eyed and worried with every minute.

As the day warmed and the fog began to dissipate, a large drip formed on the brim of my visor, grew heavy, and fell in the mud at my feet. My heart sank into my bucket-top boots. Moisture like that could easily extinguish my match, mine and John's and every man of ours. And even if the match stayed lit, moisture could so dampen the powder that when I made to thrust the match into the pan, nothing would happen. In our training, we had learned about this. "A flash in the pan," it was called. If the priming powder got moisture in it, the match, having nothing to light, would fizzle, and there would be no firing of the weapon at the enemy. My only hope was that if it was happening to our priming powder, it was equally happening to our enemies' as well.

As the fog lifted, in its place a murder of crows circled, dipping and cawing ominously. And directly overhead giant ravens soared, their oily black plumage catching the sunlight. With their deep, sonorous voices, *Krok-krok-krok*, they mocked us as they plunged and wheeled with anticipation.

My forebodings were suddenly interrupted. Our drums rumbled a command. We were to advance. I felt my childhood inclination toward swooning coming over me. We, John and I, did what we were ordered, marched several hundred yards closer to the enemy, one booted-tread at a time, carrying ourselves ever closer to our imminent peril, so I feared.

As we advanced, I heard the faint ruffling of the Royalist signal drummers. Simultaneously, King Charles' infantry advanced, and took up a close position, no more than a musket-shot directly in front of us. My heart thundered beneath the thick leather of my buff coat. I could see the whites of the eyes of our enemy, their red sashes tied across their bellies; their muskets, pistols, pikes, and halberds—real soldiers with real weapons forming a line directly in front of ours, muskets primed and ready, coming on toward the middle of our infantry.

Our infantry captain gave the order. We, the Parliament of Foot, we were to ready ourselves.

I cannot fully express my terror when first I saw men directly in front of me, left eye pinched shut, right eye wide and grim sighting down their musket barrels at us, at me.

"Present!"

In the suspended instant of waiting, I felt my miserable and all-too-short life passing before my eyes, and I so longed to escape what would follow.

"Give fire!"

Bursts of flame erupted from hundreds of gaping barrels aimed at the middle of our line, a cloud of blue smoke following, and a deafening rumble of molten lead strafing through our position.

There had been no lack in Sergeant Worthington's efforts to train us for this instant and the inevitability of casualties in close pitched battle. There is simply no way for one to be fully prepared for the cries of pain, the severed limbs, the clutching of throats, and the life blood of real men being spilled in the sod at our feet.

Our captain shouted the command. We were to return fire, those of us who were yet able to do so.

"Present! Give fire!"

I learned that however disciplined—however well-trained, however well-commanded—for the infantry soldier, war is chaos. Without regimented discipline, not one of us could hold the line and persist in giving and receiving volley fire at close range with an enemy.

After discharging our muskets, we were ordered to drop onto our left knee, as we had been trained, while the line behind us advanced into firing position. My hands trembling, I managed to prime and reload my musket. There was no time to wonder if I had maimed or killed any of the enemy—such wondering would haunt my dreams for years to come.

Wave upon wave, Royalist infantry fired and advanced, coming on with a vengeance, at last making a breach in the center of our infantry, we resorting to employing our muskets as cudgels in face-to-face and hand-to-hand combat, the bodies of our fallen lying face down in the turf.

"Hold fast!" I knew it for the gravelly voice of Sergeant Worthington, steadying us, encouraging us to stand firm against an enemy hell-bent on making a breach in our defenses.

From my tiny plot of blood-stained earth in that battlefield that day, I confess, I had no idea what was going on. I merely followed the commands I was trained by Sergeant Worthington to follow: Advance, present, give fire, reload, stand ready, advance, present, give fire—and do so until ordered to halt, or until by searing lead, or the slashing blow of a Royalist cavalry sword, I was no longer able to follow orders, cut down, out of combat, wounded or dead.

It is a bewildering puzzle to fight in a battle of such magnitude. I felt I was but one tiny piece, and encircled by the chaos of noise, the thundering of cannon, the collective thunder of volley fire after volley fire, from both ours and their infantry of foot, the choking of blue smoke, the metallic stench of saltpeter hanging heavy in the air, the shouts of command, the cries of the wounded and dying, the stench of blood, the screams of horses flailing in their death throes.

Gradually, something began to change. I would only learn later the precise details of that shift in momentum and its several causes. While both General Ireton's cavalry and we in General Skippon's infantry had taken casualties, just when it looked like Prince Rupert and King Charles' force would break through and scatter our men of foot, the cavalry of the New Model Army of Oliver Cromwell charged against the combined Royalist force, scattering men and horse before them.

King Charles and his commander attempted to rally their troops for a counterattack. But when Cromwell's cavalry again descended upon them, they turned and fled the field.

When the dust began to settle, there lay seven hundred Royalist infantry dead, their bodies contorted and dismembered from cannon and musket lead, and the cleaving strokes of cavalry swords. The ravens and crows were now joined by red kites and buzzards, all descending for the feast.

Greater loss to the Royalist cause, however, were the 5,000 men who surrendered themselves to Lord-General Fairfax and gave themselves up to the Parliamentary cause as prisoners. Additionally, the king lost all of his cannons, 9,000 weapons: muskets, swords, pikes, and halberds; and wagon-loads of provisions intended for the feeding of his now scattering army.

Fleeing for their lives, King Charles and his commander rode twenty miles north back to the walled city of Leicester recently taken by the Royalists troops and brutally plundered. Conscripting every male from sixteen to sixty to replenish his army, frantically, Charles set about to prepare for the inevitable siege that would follow.

After our dead were booked and buried, a task so gruesome I do not care to dwell upon it in my narrative, I cannot fully express my great relief upon being reunited with John Bunyan and our good sergeant, all of us counted amongst the survivors of the Battle of Naseby.

That weary night, we all lying exhausted about the charcoal fire hard by the battlefield, too fatigued to speak, it was taciturn Sergeant Worthington who broke the silence. His words, as only later events would prove, were so prophetic, I shall never forget them as long as I live. And neither, methinks, shall John Bunyan.

"God hath spared thee," said he, gazing unblinking into the coals, "for a far greater deliverance."

14

Narrow Escape

I have heard fighting men claim that they know because they were there. Theirs is only in the most limited sense a reliable line of reasoning. But if a man for having been there claims to know the grand movements of divisions and armies because he was there, it is an absurd claim, known to be so by anyone who has actually fought in a battle, such as John Bunyan and I fought on June 14, 1645, at Naseby.

A great deal of what I herein record about the decisive battle of the entire war and its immediate aftermath, I only learned in retrospect. I have heard it said that one cannot see the forest for the trees. Well, in battle, one cannot see the whole for being so immediately engaged in its parts, that is to say, in one very small part thereof.

Holding the line where I stood shaking in my bucket-top boots, my wide eyes were clouded and watering with the smoke. What remained of my hearing was assaulted by the cries and rumblings of war. It was impossible for me to know anything of what was going on more than a few yards from the bloody turf on which my feet were planted, still less did I know what was afoot in our cavalry, or in the other divisions of our infantry. Of the machinations of our enemy's army, her tactics and stratagems, I knew nothing.

Hard-fought-and-won-battle that Naseby was, there was to be no resting for our infantry. June 15, the Lord's Day as our Puritan chaplains and commanders called it, was nevertheless, in the New Model Army, a day for marching and fighting. Lord-General Fairfax and Lieutenant-General Cromwell believed that the ox of our Parliamentary cause was in the proverbial ditch.

After morning prayers, the reading of Holy Writ, and the singing of a Psalm, we were ordered to break camp and be on the march within the hour. If we did not press our advantage in pursuit of King Charles and his Royalist army, he would rearm himself and prolong the conflict.

"'We must take the current when it serves,'" quoted John upon hearing of our orders, "'or lose our ventures.'"

As I watched the cavalry ride by on their fine horses, I grimaced at my aching feet. We were to march all twenty miles on foot, and arrive prepared to lay siege to the walled city. I knew only the barest rudiments of siege warfare, and wondered what role John and I might be tasked to play in the endeavor. We would soon find out.

When our regiment of foot arrived at the battered walls of Leicester, on Tuesday, June 17, Lord-General Fairfax's surrender order had been rejected. In defiance, the Royalist commander had placed snipers along the battlements of the walled town, snipers with orders to shoot all Puritans on sight. His terms of surrender roundly rejected, Fairfax ordered his Parliamentary army to commence siege warfare against the beleaguered town.

Due to losses at Naseby, John and I were temporarily assigned to assist in raising a battery of cannon on the Raw Dykes, a strategic high ground, well suited to bombard the now-Royalist stronghold into submission. It was from Colonel Rainsborough, in charge of the operation, that we learned of the ironies of what we were engaged in.

"It was but eighteen days ago," said Rainsborough, in our hearing, "when doomed Leicester fell into the brutal hands of the popish king and his Royalists supporters. The vicious cruelties enacted against the people of this poor place will go down in infamy, and be a black mark against the king who ordered such pitiless crimes. Ah, but we shall, by God's grace, give the devil his due, and we shall do so for this devilish king with his own cannons."

Colonel Rainsborough said the latter while patting with affection the massive barrel of a culverin, a long-range siege cannon. He went on to explain that the cannons we were readying for the bombardment were Royalist cannons seized at Naseby, and that the battery on Raw Dykes was the exact same spot where Charles had ordered the Royalist bombardment of the city less than three weeks before in the first siege of Leicester.

"This, the second siege of this beleaguered city," he continued, "will inflict the final blow to the Royalist cause, God be praised. After Naseby and our liberation of Leicester, Charles and his cause are doomed."

We were to learn that there is a good deal of digging involved in raising a battery of cannons. Before long, it felt very much like John and I were to be the chief diggers. As we wielded our spades, John would pause from time to time and gaze at the walled city, with that dreamy look that often came into his eyes when his imagination was aflame. I wondered what fantastical mischief he was scheming in that ever-mysterious mind of his. Only time would tell.

Later that evening, exhausted from our task in raising a battery for the bombardment, just as we were ready to collapse in our tent and sleep, an infantry captain halted in front of our tent. Like good soldiers, weary though we were, we scrambled to our feet at attention.

Recall that I have described the physical appearance of John Bunyan as he was, a sturdy fellow, broad of shoulder, and nearly a head taller than the average adult man. I can only assume that it was for this reason that the captain's eyes fell upon John.

"I am short of men for sentinel duty at the wall," said he. "I need replacements. What is your name, son?"

"I am called John Bunyan, sir."

"And you, lad?" said the captain turning to me.

"I am called Harry Wylie, sir," said I.

"John Bunyan," said he, "and Harry Wylie," said he, "gather your weapons and follow me."

Inwardly I groaned. We had marched twenty weary miles from Naseby, John and I. We had spent a long day at the battery, entrenching cannons for the bombardment; and now we were to march back and forth through the long night, twenty pounds of musket on our weary shoulders, all night, enemy snipers lining the crenellation of the wall?

Without a word, nevertheless, we began gathering our weapons.

"The lads, they're weary, unfit for sentinel duty."

It was Sergeant Worthington's gravelly voice, his tent, as always, pitched a boot-width next to ours.

"Labored hard at the battery, did they."

Our good sergeant had already taken up his musket, his bandolier of premeasured gunpowder flasks slung over one shoulder, and his leather shot pouch over the other.

"I'll go."

The captain looked Sergeant Worthington over from head to toe. "Very good of you, sergeant. Relieve my sentinel before the Newarke Wall, posthaste."

The captain turned and disappeared into the growing darkness.

Without another word, Sergeant Worthington put a hand on each of our shoulders, like a father would do to his sons. I shall never forget the affectionate look he gave us that fateful evening, a flicker of light reflecting from the glow of his cooking fire in his kindly gray eyes.

There was a hush in the air that night, as if both armies were holding their breath before the cataclysm of noise and mayhem that the bombardment would surely cause next morning. Relieved of sentinel duty and exhausted, John and I rolled ourselves in our blankets and fell into a deep sleep.

I do not know what hour it was. But I awoke with a start. Piercing the silence of that night, the retort of a single musket shot reechoed off the medieval walls of that ill-fated city.

My heart thundering in my breast, John awake and hard on my heels, we ran to our front line before the Newarke Wall of the city. We ran as if knowing.

I stopped in my tracks. There he lay, flat on his back, a hole the size of a musket ball in his forehead. I fell onto my knees at his side. John did the same. We each took up a calloused and scarred hand in our own. Bewildered by it all, too sorrowful for words, we held his hands as they grew cold in our own.

15

Lamentation

Sergeant Ezra Worthington was laid to rest and given full military honors by our regiment. John Gibbs, our young chaplain, delivered the sermon based on the text from the Geneva Bible: "I am the resurrection and the life: he that believeth in me, though he were dead yet shall he live. And whosoever liveth, and believeth in me, shall never die." After which reading, Mr. Gibbs impressed upon each of our hearts, most earnestly, that we, every man of us, believe in Jesus Christ who alone is the resurrection and the life. I stared unblinking at the unmoving corpse of that good man laid out before us, tears streaming unabated down my cheeks.

It is impossible fully to express in words the thrilling anguish of thousands of men at arms, joining their voices, voices fortified in the tragedies and triumphs of warfare, voices now united in the singing of a Psalm of lamentation.

Bitter tears of lamentation
Are my food by night and day.
In my deep humiliation,
"Where is now thy God?" they say.
Oh, my soul's poured out in me
When I bring to memory...

My voice quavered and then broke down like an old cartwheel. I was forced to halt my singing as the Psalm brought to my memory the goodness of Sergeant Ezra Worthington. I lacked the words needed to express my grief at his taking off, and at his willfully doing so in our place. I felt that there were deep waters here, but did not then know how to plumb their depths.

Of the war, there was much to tell. Of our part in it, there was little else to tell. The bombardment in the second siege of Leicester began at first light on June 18, 1645. We, John and me, took some pride in the fact that the battery we helped raise on Raw Dykes made a breach in the wall before the morning was out. By day's end, the Royalist army had surrendered without condition.

By their surrender, our Parliamentary army seized fourteen cannons, 2,000 muskets and other weapons, fifty barrels of gunpowder, 500 horses, and ox carts and carriages filled with provisions to feed an army. But no longer for the feeding of King Charles' army.

The king was nowhere to be seen. It was reported that he was on the run. The tide of the war had clearly turned, and he must certainly have known that in a short time the war would be ended, and so would end his tyrannical reign, and soon enough would end his life, his miserable head lifted from his shoulders for all to see in London in 1649. Meanwhile, one-time Lieutenant-General Oliver Cromwell would be made Lord Protector to serve at the behest of Parliament.

Hostilities finally at an end, John Bunyan and me along with him, ever at his heels, were mustered out of General Skippon's Parliamentary Soldiers of Foot midsummer of 1647.

Whereupon, leaving our regiment behind us, much affected by our military service, we set out on the highway back to our humble homes in Elstow. Our lives would never be the same.

16

Ailing Pots and Pans

I would have thought that after all we had experienced together in the war, John and me, seeing the dead and dying all about us in the field at Naseby, and the great mercy of Sergeant Worthington's self-sacrifice on our behalf—I say, I would have thought that John Bunyan would be softened, averse to returning to his blasphemous ways. But it was not so. Ever the rebel against God, John seemed to grow still more careless of his salvation, though he discovered new and creative ways to engage in that rebellion, as I was soon to find out.

Six months after our return from the war, it was while at his tinkering trade that I began to see a change overpowering him. Bearing in mind that I had come to despair in the whole notion of men actually changing, as I have said. This being more of a change in tactics than a change in moral practices.

On a chilly morning in early January, 1648, John hoisted the family anvil into the turf three doors down from Elstow's coaching inn. "Pots to mend, knives to grind—any work for the tinker?"

Then, blowing warmth into his fingers, he commenced playing a merry tune on his tin fiddle. Winter day that it was, a young woman presented John with a copper kettle that needed repairing. As he chatted with her at his anvil, I observed a slight flush rising on John's ruddy cheeks, and wondered at the cause.

Two days later, the same young woman presented John with another cooking vessel in need of repair. There was more flushing of his cheeks, and a faraway expression in his gaze as he conversed with the young woman.

Less than a week later, the very same young woman presented another battered pot to the tinker. I marveled that any family could have so many cooking vessels under one roof. I watched closely as John gazed at the young woman, and I drew close to discover the cause of his strange behaviors. He entirely ignored me, as if I was not there, did not exist.

All the while, John continued the steady tapping of his hammer on the tin, his eyes transfixed on the face of the young woman, his mouth sagging open in an adoring fashion, all the while his hammer rising and falling as if on its own reflex.

I saw it coming and winced at the sight.

Thud!

Not minding his business, John had brought his hammer down squarely onto his thumbnail. Knowing what a prodigious blasphemer he was, I fully expected an eloquent string of profanity that would make a seaman blush, and a stomping contrivance of rage accompanying his harangue. I had seen the same before.

But there was nothing. Blanching with pain, his face grew ruddier than usual, and he cradled his mangled digit in his other hand, but nothing else. No cursing, no swearing, no vulgar expostulations. Nothing.

The young woman was filled with sympathy for his smashed thumb and told him so more than once. He accepted her ministrations with deference and gallantry.

Later that day, I questioned him about these strange occurrences.

He gave me a withering look, as if to say, there was nothing in the slightest strange about his behavior. "Harry, my friend, I mean to enter," said he, "the holy state of matrimony, and public blasphemy does not befit a man in such a station."

I was all astonishment at his words. "You mean to leave off cursing and swearing, then?"

"As if I had never sworn or been a swearer," said he, his eyelids piously fluttering over the whites of his eyes, "as the good book says."

His words sounded vaguely familiar, and I racked my brain trying to recall where it said such a thing but to no avail.

One week later, and the strangest sight appeared ambulating along the Elstow High Street. John walked along encumbered with the burdens of his trade, his bag of hammers and rivets, and the like, and his anvil perched upon his shoulder. This was in no way strange, but in his free hand he carried an open book, reading therein as he walked. We had been through much together in the war, and I had heard tell that some men exhibited strange behaviors after battle. As his comrade in arms, I felt the obligation of intervention.

"John, whatever are you reading?"

He signaled me for silence, and continued walking and reading, apparently until he had finished the page. I fell in at his heels, as was my wont.

"A book," he replied at last, keeping his damaged thumb in his place, while turning the book so I could observe its spine.

"'The Plain Man's Pathway to Heaven,'" I read thereupon.

"By Arthur Dent," he added, "minister in Shoebury in Essex. Penned in 1601."

"Wherever did you acquire such a book?" I knew that books were expensive, and the son of a tinker, just entering on his trade, could little afford to spend his few shillings on a book.

He reddened slightly, cleared his throat, and thrust out his chin defensively.

"Aha, aha, I see it all clearly," said I. "You're a very devil, John. It's hers, is it not?"

"Whose?" said he, in studied bewilderment.

"You know whose. The fair young woman. The one with the myriad of ailing pots and pans. So, she has books too, does she?"

"Her father does," said he. "She is ever devoted to her father, is she. I mean to read all of his books."

"All of them? How many books does he have?" I asked with some astonishment to hear that anyone living in poor Elstow could own so many books.

"Two books," said he. "And I mean to read them both."

Narrowing my eyes, I looked askance at him. "I know what you're up to, John. You may be able to fool them, but I know your contrivances."

John had a manner of sulking when he felt offended, and at my accusatory words he had cloaked his countenance in one of his pouting expressions. I snatched the book from him and read aloud.

"'Wherein every man may surely see whether he be saved or damned.'" I looked at John. "Well, my friend, you have no need of reading further. I for certain, if not the whole shire, know of which company you belong."

His hurt expression deepened.

I read on. "Aha, here in the contents, it reads, 'Swearing, and the punishment thereof, excuses for swearing, causes of swearing, remedies against swearing.' And just above that, 'Contempt of the gospel a grievous sin.'" I snapped the book closed. "Are you certain you want to read this book? It sounds to my ears like the author has herein written a full and complete biography of John Bunyan." I laughed heartily at my own wit.

John did not join me. He snatched the book back, opened to the page he had been reading, and continued walking, walking and reading, burdened with the tools of his trade upon his back.

Two weeks later, John Bunyan did what he said he was about to do, entered into the holy state of matrimony with the beautiful and virtuous young woman from Elstow, the rite solemnized by our parson Christopher Hall in the nave of the great abbey church.

Knowing John for the villain that deep down he was, I pitied the poor lass now wedded to such a man as he.

17

Off with His Head

Meanwhile, revolutionary changes were afoot in the realm, changes that would have far-reaching consequences in the future life of John Bunyan, as I shall hereafter relate.

Since grasping King Henry VIII declared himself the supreme head of the church in the year of our Lord, 1534, the sovereign had ruled not merely over civil matters but equally ruled supreme over matters of the church. Whomsoever the monarch be, he or she was the head of the church.

During the absolute reign of Catholic-leaning Charles I, now held in prison, shortly to have his head lopped off at the block, the authority of the monarch over the church was greatly expanded by his Archbishop William Laud. The tyrannical archbishop's relentless crushing of all unauthorized preaching throughout England and Scotland was a major factor in the recent clash of arms between Parliament and the Crown in the English Civil War.

But it was not only Puritans and Parliamentarians who had little affection for the monstrous policies of Laud. Even the king's own jester created mocking verse at the brutal fellow:

Give great praise to the Lord
And little Laud to the devil.

A clever play on words, Laud also being the Latin for praise, which set me to wondering how John Bunyan, with his ready wit and poetic proclivities, might have made a fitting court jester, that is, in another life. But not in this one, there being no record of a son of the tinker class being elevated to court, however clever and profane of wits he may be.

I return to my narrative. So, in 1642, when Parliament took up arms against Charles, the king fled London and set up his court in Oxford. By his doing so, the Anglican Church, with the monarch as the head of said church, no longer existed. It was dissolved just as Charles his own self had previously dissolved Parliament.

Hence, Parliament called the wisest of Puritan and Covenanter theologians and preachers from throughout the realm to gather in Westminster Abbey, there to form a new and Reformed confession of faith.

The Westminster Divines, as these able men were called, laid the foundation for a church over which no king or sovereign would have any authority. There were to be no kings or their strutting bishops and archbishops ruling the church. The King of kings alone would have his rightful place as sovereign over his church. Ministers and elders who adhered to what the Scriptures principally taught as summarized in the Westminster Confession of Faith would be duly trained and ordained to preach. But there would be no longer any oath of allegiance to a monarch as head of the church, and no bishop would have authority over a man's call to preach the gospel.

Just as King Charles would have his head lopped off at Whitehall in 1649, so, by these changes, the headship of any monarch over the church had been lopped off—or so it then seemed.

I herein expostulate these matters because they would be of the gravest consequence in the future life of John Bunyan, as I shall relate forthwith.

18

Bells and Blindness

I n these early months of John Bunyan's wedded life, I was forced to observe that the company of the fairer sex had exerted a restraining influence on the man. He was much taken with his young bride, and his devotion to her fueled his determination, by the exercise of his own will, to make himself worthy of this virtuous and lovely woman, poor peasant though she be.

"These two books of her father's, Harry," said he, "but still more, my dear wife's tender virtues, have begot within me the desire to reform my vicious life, and so I shall."

He told me this himself. And I observed for a time his public exertion to make himself appear pious and thereby appear worthy of such as she. "Harry, hold me to account," said he. "I am giving up forever my swearing, and all such other public behaviors as are not befitting to a man of my station."

I confess, I laughed in his face at his declaration, and dared him to be more than a poor, painted hypocrite, even if all the world thought him to be otherwise. I knew what he was deep down, and would ever be.

Not surprisingly, I had little conversation with John Bunyan for some considerable months after my bold words defying his grandiose resolves.

It was in middle July of the year 1650 that word circulated around the village of Elstow that John was a father. I shook my head in wonder at the news. What kind of a father would such a one as he become? I felt certain I knew the answer.

On the Lord's Day, July 20, 1650, the happy couple presented for holy baptism at the abbey font their firstborn, a girl child they called Mary. We, all of us, had made our squealing debut in the chilly waters of that medieval font. Our parson Christopher Hall baptized little Mary, "In the name of the Father, and of the Son, and of the Holy Ghost." And the little wet one duly responded with a hiccup and blood-chilling wail.

After the benediction, the service ended, I observed John standing at the base of the bell tower a longing expression upon his face.

I knew his love of bell ringing, and imagined that he had reasoned that on such a happy occasion, ringing of the great bells was fitting. The oaken door to the tower was opened, and I followed as he entered.

I watched in the dim light as that irrepressible look came over his features. His jaw slack, his eyes upturned and riveted on the great bells suspended on ancient oak crossbeams above us. I'd seen that look often enough in our youth when some new caper was afoot in his imagination.

"Harry, you pull this one," said he, handing me a rope. "I'll pull the number five bell," he continued, but his voice quavered as he said it.

"Alright, then," said I, awaiting his first pull.

But nothing happened. No merry clanging of the number five bell. I had seen him many times before, his eyes wild with enthusiasm, rising and falling with energy as he pulled, his hair lifting and splaying madly with each pull, incontinent exuberance glowing on his cheeks. But he was frozen, statue-like, his face pale and blanching.

"John, what ails you?"

He swallowed hard and glanced backward at the doorway, then upward again at the great bells. I had observed it increasing in him since the war, his fear of confined spaces, of being hemmed in, of being restrained in any fashion.

Looking my way, his eyes wide, as if an idea had suddenly occurred to him, he backed toward the doorway, hand-over-hand, keeping hold of the rope. Achieving the knot at the end of the bell pull, just outside beyond the tower doorway, he commenced ringing, the rope sawing on the stone lintel, his shoes grinding in the gravel underfoot on the path as he exerted himself with each pull.

Shaking my head in wonderment at his odd behavior, I pulled my bell in turn, and the steeple fairly rocked with the peels of those ancient bells. Over and again we pulled.

When at last we had exhausted ourselves, I rejoined him in the church yard. "What plagues you, John?" I asked. "Why pull the bells from the doorway and not from within the bell tower as we've always done?"

John's face grew sober again. "Have you looked closely at those bells, Harry? Have you calculated how much each of them must weigh? Tons and tons, and the old beams holding them up?" He paused, a wild look in his eyes, as if he was seeing something I could not see.

"*Old* beams, they are, Harry. What if one of them cracked under the strain and broke?" said he. "What then? The bells, they would plummet down and crush me. God knows, Harry, I deserve it as a judgment for my sins."

He had a point. He having been the ringleader, the chief vulgarian of the sins of our youth, he was correct; his sins were far greater than my own. Try as I might, I could find no words to console him.

We walked together in silence back to the abbey, where his wife and the women of the village were cooing over little Mary. He hesitated, looking back over his shoulder at the bell tower.

"I won't do it again, Harry," said he. "As we were ringing of them, did you feel it?"

"Feel what?"

"The tower itself a-swaying with the bells? No, I shall never ring the bells again, for fear the very steeple itself will fall upon my head."

Hoping he didn't detect my scrutiny, I looked at him from the corner of my eye as our feet crunched beneath us on the gravel path. I wondered, was the lead leeching into his small beer from his pewter mug, or was it something else? Had he gone brain sick from our experiences in the war?

We rejoined his wife and daughter, and I turned back toward the village. As I passed three or four women speaking in low tones, I overheard their talk.

"I don't think either of 'em realizes it," said one in guarded tones, glancing back at the young couple and daughter.

"'Tis such a pity," said another.

I slowed my pace to hear more.

"I don't 'ave the 'eart to tell 'em."

"Nor do I," said another. "Who's to tell a mother 'er little one will never see? Poor thing's blind as a bat."

19

Another World

I saw John Bunyan making his way down Church End a week later, the accoutrements of his trade upon his back, as always, and an open book in his hand. More and more he traveled about the countryside in this odd fashion.

"Greetings, John," I called, falling in step at his side.

As before, he held up his hand while he finished his reading.

I marveled at his manner of travel. After the Roman legions left a few years back, our English roads and byways have been none too level, straight, or narrow. Traveling about in such a blind fashion, it's a wonder he didn't grievously bedaub himself with mire in the many potholes and ditches.

After a few moments, he glanced up at me.

"What are you reading of this time?" I asked.

He turned the book so I could read its title from the spine.

"Holy Bible," I read. "Where did you get it?"

"The parson lent it to me," said John.

"Have you discovered yet another verse to live by therein?"

He reopened the book, cleared his throat, and commenced reading aloud, intoning as if he were a bishop: "'The labor of fools wearies him, for he does not even know how to go to the city of God.'"

"'The labor of fools,' is it?" said I, eyeing him with a wink. But he made no response. As he made to resume his reading, I commented, "'Tis a big book. Wherein do you read?"

"I read mostly in the historical parts," said he. "I find great pleasure in reading the historical parts. But the epistles of Paul and such Scriptures in the later pages, they're harder to understand. Make little sense to my way of thinking, do they. So, I read the historical parts and find great pleasure in the Law of Moses and the commandments, which I have made great resolves to keep, every one of them."

He paused, appraising me. I felt he was calculating whether the likes of me could find pleasure in any of its parts. Then he launched into one of his lectures, expostulating on the biblical text, posing hypothetical questions, answering those same questions with erudite dexterity, or he appeared to imagine so of himself.

I'd had enough and held up my hand for him to stop. "I seem to recall a different John Bunyan," said I, putting a hand on my hip and doing my best to imitate his cavalier manners. "How did you put it then? 'What is the Bible? Give me a ballad, a newsbook, George on Horseback, or Bevis of Southampton. Give me some book that teaches curious arts, or that tells old fables; but away with Holy Scripture!' Thusly do I recall another man declaring."

"Did I say that?"

I assured him that he had said precisely that.

"Surely, Harry, you know that much of what I say, I say in jest."

I wanted to remind him that he was a common tinker, and, worse yet, the village blasphemer. What business did he have yammering on about theological matters as if he were the prince of Puritans himself? But though I held my tongue, he did not.

"You should amend your ways, Harry," he continued, turning his head, his chin up, his eyes looking back and down at me, "amend your ways as I have done mine. Persist in the way thou goest, hear me, Harry, and thou shalt have wearisomeness, painfulness, hunger, perils, nakedness, sword, lions, dragons, darkness, and, in a word, death, and what not."

I looked at the man, mouth agape. I considered reminding him that he, a painted hypocrite, was the very paragon of profanity, but as I grappled for the right words, he persisted in his call to my reformation.

"These are religious times, Harry, and you ought to say and sing very devoutly with the foremost of the religious in our day, as I have done."

"John! I know you by the back, like no other," said I, when once I found my tongue. "As you have done? Humph! Cleaning the outside of the cup, are we, all whilst retaining of your wicked ways inside."

At the first he seemed offended at my observation, but then he looked heavenward, as if crying for patience with such a one as I. After which, fortified by divine assistance, he carried on with his homily on Moses and the commandments, and my reformation thereby.

"Harry," said he, "why do you swear and curse thus?"

"Why?" With a laugh, I retorted, "I was taught thus by the master craftsman of the art!"

"But what will become of you," said he, "if you die in this condition?"

Though he seemed in earnest, I replied in jest. "What would the devil do for company, if it were not for such as I am?"

It was nearly a week later that I had further discourse with him. He was trudging along the London Road after a day of plying his trade in Bedford, but I noticed he had no book opened in his hand. I approached and asked him why he had left off reading.

He ran a calloused hand across his forehead before making reply; if I was not mistaken, there appeared to be a tremor in his hand as he did so. After which, he began talking. He was ever a great one for talking, was John Bunyan, ever chewing the cud, was he, but seldom splitting the hoof, none that I ever saw.

"I was making to set up shop," he began, his voice sober, "along St. Cuthbert's Street, you know the place. When on the verge of calling out my trade, I overheard the strangest thing."

He leaned closer toward me, in that conspiratorial fashion of his, then continued.

"Hard by my anvil, there were three or four poor women sitting at a door in the sun, and talking about the things of God. You know me, Harry, ever a brisk talker myself in the matters of religion. So, I gave heed to better hear what they said."

He paused in his narrative, lowering his anvil to the ground beside the road. Sighing heavily, he sat down on the bottom step of a stile for climbing over the stone dyke that ran along that stretch of roadway. I joined him.

"And, what did they say?"

"I heard the words, Harry, but I understood not. They were far above, out of my reach. Their talk was about a new birth, the work of God on their hearts, also how they were convinced of their miserable state by nature. They talked how God had visited their souls with his love in the Lord Jesus, and with what words and promises they had been refreshed, comforted, and supported against the temptations of the devil.

"Moreover, they reasoned of the temptations of Satan in particular; and told each other by which ones they had been afflicted, and how they were borne up under his assaults. They also discoursed of their own wretchedness of heart, of their unbelief; and did condemn, slight, and abhor their own righteousness, as filthy and insufficient to do them any good."

He broke off, his eyes following a murder of crows down the way arguing over the remains of some unfortunate creature, crushed by a cartwheel.

"Did you join in their talk?"

Hurling a stone at the crows, he shook his head. "They were far above me, Harry, out of my reach," said he. "Methought they spake as if joy did make them speak; they spake with such pleasantness of Scripture language, and with such appearance of grace in all they said, that they were to me as if they had found a new world, as if they were people that dwelt alone, and were not to be reckoned amongst their neighbors."

Drawing in breath, I readied myself to mock and curse the talk of such foolish women, but I halted. John's hands trembled as he hoisted his anvil, once again, upon his broad shoulders. With his dreaming-whilst-standing-up look in the eyes, he murmured good day to me, and turned his steps toward Elstow and his home.

I watched him grow smaller, the cart tracks in the road trailing serpent-like behind him. I was bewildered by the man John Bunyan, ever hot and cold, ever fair and foul, ever profane and pious. Who was he? What was he becoming? He was now but a tiny dejected pin-prick disappearing around a bend in the highway. I scowled after him.

20

Be Puddles!

I t was in the harvest time of 1650, while I was
laboring with my sickle alongside my father cutting
rye from our landlord's field that I witnessed a most
strange occurrence on the road hard by the field in which
we labored.

Unbending myself and wiping the sweat from my
brow, I had suddenly caught sight of the head of a man
bobbing along just visible above the hawthorn hedge
lining the field. I welcomed the momentary distraction
from my labors, and drew closer to investigate.

Through the woven branches of the hawthorn I
caught a glimpse of the man. Sure enough, John Bunyan
it was, bowed down under his tinker's tools making his
way along the road. So preoccupied was he that he was
wholly unmindful of my presence. I knew this to be
normal for the man; ever the dreamer, was he, so often
carried off with extravagant fancies, mesmerized by his
own imagination.

His must have been a weary day of labor, for he suddenly halted and unburdened himself, yet remained standing between the cart tracks in the middle of the road.

I have expressed my relief at not being born into the tinker class, as was John Bunyan. This was largely on account of my having once attempted to carry the heavy burden of his anvil upon my shoulder. Thereafter, I grew more grateful at my father's calling to the farming life; and never, thereafter, envied him his.

On the verge of hailing him through the hedgerow, my words were suddenly arrested by John's own words. He was speaking, yet there was no man nearby—that is, none that he knew of. Skulking on tiptoe, I moved as silently as I could to a place where the tangled branches of the hawthorn were thinner, and thereby allowed me a clearer sight of the man. I believe that I hoped, at his expense, to discover some entertainment thereby, as proved to be very much the case.

He had by this time bent his knees and extended his arms toward an object in front of him on the road, and stood unmoving as if in a trance. I strained to see what prank or madness he was about. Suddenly, his hands fell to his sides and he turned and strode directly toward my place of concealment on the other side of the hedge.

Unaware as he was of my presence, I prepared myself to give him a fright, and amuse myself at his startled reaction. I filled my lungs to cry out as if I were a hobgoblin, but at the same instant, John fell to his knees. I hesitated, studying the man.

At first his lips moved silently, but then he gave it tongue. "Oh, that I knew the truth and the way to heaven and glory," cried he. "Oh Lord, your Word is precious to me, yet it tells me that all things are given by thee, Oh Lord. It tells me that I must have faith, but it tells me that thou alone must give faith to me. Those in a faithless state have neither rest nor quiet in their souls, and I fear that I have neither, and am loathe to fall quite into despair. Show me, oh Lord, how may I know if I have faith?"

There was more to his praying, but my mind was suddenly loathe, though blasphemer that I was, to play a prank on a man in such earnest conversation with the Almighty.

At last the undulations of his anguished praying fell silent, and he rose to his feet again. Just as he turned, I sensed a new resolve on his features, though they were rather spidery as seen through the tangle of hawthorn that divided us.

Once back on the road, he rummaged in his things and produced his Bible. I strained to hear as he read therein, but a breeze snatched away much of the reading. I caught only bits and pieces: "If ye have faith… and ye say to this mountain, be moved… it shall be moved… into the sea." But it made little sense to me.

He set aside his Bible and resumed his trance-like posture, his knees bent, his arms raised, eyes pinched tight shut. What on earth was he playing at? I held my breath.

"Be dry!" he shouted, flinging his arms forward and down at the muddy ruts in the road. He stood prone for an instant. Cautiously, he opened first one eye and then the other. Then he fell on his hands and knees, not in supplication, but in close inspection of some detail I could not see.

With a heavy sigh, he rose to his feet, and turned to the ridge in between the cart ruts. After resuming his stance, arms aloft, he cried, "Be puddles!" and apparently for good measure, he repeated his command, still louder the second time. "*Be puddles!*"

It came over me, as I stared in wonder at his performance; he may be past all hope. The hobgoblins had fully daunted his spirit. Or perhaps the war had done it, unhinged his brains, his mind now and forever the mind of a castaway. I pitied the man and longed for the carefree madness of his youth.

21

Four Last Things

Though I had become a firm believer in the unchangeability of men, I could not deny the changing of the times. Time passed, one year marching onward into the next, and the next after that one. Meanwhile, there were many changes afoot in England.

After Charles was beheaded, his son in exile, Lieutenant-General Oliver Cromwell was made Lord Protector of the realm in 1653, and Parliamentary politics and Puritan preaching flourished throughout the land.

Meanwhile, John Bunyan and I were expected to fulfill our callings in a responsible way for the good of the community and our families; hence, our paths crossed not as often nor as riotously as they had in our youth.

I marveled in these short years to observe the Bunyan family growing larger, with blind Mary ever at his side, her hand firmly and affectionately held in her father's, and another little girl toddling at his other side, Elizabeth by name. And two little boys followed some time thereafter, John, named after his father, and Thomas, named for his grandfather.

At the baptism of young Thomas, I observed John's wife across the medieval font. I had only heard that delivering a baby could be a painful activity and could result in physical discomforts that might not go hastily away after being delivered of the child itself. Not having any direct experience of these mysterious matters, I was left to my powers of observation. Her complexion was that of yellowed parchment paper, her cheeks cadaverous, and her posture bent, as if she continued still in her labor pains.

Ever attentive to his wife's ill health, John said little to me about Mary's blindness, but I observed with wonder his tender devotion to his eldest daughter's every need.

One market day on the Elstow Green, in a lull in his tinkering, I happened by and drew near. Sitting at his side, I listened as he related an extraordinary tale to me; ever the storyteller was he.

"I often returned to St. Cuthbert's Street to listen to those godly women, did I," he began. "I told them of my fears. My fear that the day of mercy had passed. That, blasphemer that ever I had been, I had gone too far, had committed the unpardonable sin, blasphemy against the Holy Ghost. And my fear that, faithless man that I know myself to be, I was not amongst the elect.

"They heard me with patience, but not knowing how to console me in my fears, they introduced me to their pastor, a man of the name John Gifford, parson of the independent chapel at St. John's across the Ouse in Bedford, you know it."

I assured him that I did.

"Mr. Gifford invited me to his vestry where he most attentively listened as I recounted my fears. When I had at last unburdened myself to the man, he then told me a story.

"Major John Gifford had been an officer in the Civil War—but on the other side, a Royalist. By his own account he was a notorious blasphemer, a debauched drunkard, and an inveterate gambler, though not a very skillful one, as I shall relate."

I interjected with a laughed, "He sounds like another vile ruffian I have heard tell of."

John pretended not to hear. "The Earl of Norwich, ever loyal to deposed King Charles, now in prison, rallied his forces and led a rebellion against Parliament.

"On June 1 of 1648, Lord-General Fairfax confronted Norwich and his officers in one of the bloodiest final confrontations of the war—a full year, Harry, after we ourselves had mustered out of the army.

"In the foulest of weather, soaked with the drenching rain, the two armies engaged in a running battle with skirmishes throughout the town, blood mingling with the rain water and running thick in the gutters. The Royalists finally took their stand at Saint Faith's churchyard, barricading themselves, awaiting the Parliamentary assault.

"Gifford described his terror as the Puritan army came on with their battle cry 'Truth! Truth!' They did their best, but by battle's end, the Royalists had lost hundreds of men, with 1,400 surrendering themselves up to Fairfax, whose Parliamentary army had only lost eighty men.

"Major John Gifford was one of eleven officers who were detained in All Saints Church, Maidstone. Fairfax and his Puritan army showed mercy to the rank and file; but there was a war on, and for Gifford's part in the rebellion, he along with the other ten men were sentenced to the gallows.

"Harry, here's where the story gets particularly exhilarating. The night before John Gifford was to be hanged by the neck until dead, his sister appealed to the Puritan jailers for one last visit with her brother."

By the flashing in his eyes, I could see that John was warming to his own narrative. At times like these, I was prone to wonder if he was augmenting the tale with colorful bits of his own devising.

"She told her brother that she had a scheme to break him out of his confinement. He laughed. She persisted. He objected. She assured him that the Puritans would not make her go to the gallows in her brother's place; their theological principles would not allow it. With the discretion of siblings, they exchanged garments. His sister's bonnet pulled down over his debauched features, Gifford walked out of jail that night wearing her petticoat and robe."

"Imagine the jailer's surprise next morning!" said I, slapping him on the back, delighted at his telling. "Instead of a dissolute officer awaiting the noose, there was a devoted sister wearing her brother's leather buff coat and britches!"

We enjoyed a good laugh together. After which, he resumed the story.

"Hiding out as a fugitive in London, the net closing in, Gifford fled to a backwater shire, someplace of no account, where he hoped he would be safe."

"Bedford," said I.

"Indeed, you're a scholar, Harry. Still hiding his true identity, Gifford married, and began a practice as a physician, all the while continuing his drunkenness and gambling.

"Ever loyal to the debauched court of the Stuart monarchy, Gifford despised Puritans and Parliamentarians. He was a veritable Saul of Tarsus to Puritan Christians and preachers, and was determined to do anything to mock and discredit the gospel they proclaimed.

"One night after losing a prodigious amount of money at the dice, in a fit of drunken rage, Gifford made for the Bedford bridge, intending to hurl himself into the black waters of the River Great Ouse, thereby avoiding his debts by ending his miserable existence."

My mind ran suddenly back to the night John Bunyan and I nearly met our end in that same river.

"Did he do it?" I asked.

John gave me one of his withering looks, as if to say, how could he have done it, for it was Gifford alive and well who was telling the story to him?

"On the brink of doing it, Gifford felt inside his pocket. There was a pamphlet that had been given him containing writings of a Puritan by the name of Robert

Bolton. Now, Harry, mind you, Gifford was not the sort of man to be reading Puritan sermons. Not one, indeed.

"But something compelled him to do so, and he was profoundly moved in the reading of Bolton. He discovered a humble man, fervent in faith, devotion, and prayer, as if he were a child talking with his father. He was a man much consumed with the four last things." He broke off, hammer idle in his hands, gazing at the far end of the green, where stood the medieval cross.

"And what might those things be?" I urged.

"Death, judgment, hell, and heaven," continued John. "The four last things, Harry. Gifford told me of Christ, and of Bolton's devotion to his Lord. 'I feel nothing in my soul but Christ, with whom I heartily desire to be,' so wrote Bolton. Gifford was at last apprehended."

"Aha, by the law? They finally caught up with him?"

Another withering look. "No, Harry, apprehended by Christ. That's how Puritan preachers speak."

Now, I felt John Bunyan was speaking words but I understood them not, as if he too was from another world.

"John Gifford was born anew," he continued, "and threw himself into the study of the Bible, guided by the writings of Bolton and other Puritans. Two years later he was called to be parson of St. John's independent chapel, in the vestry of which he told me this tale."

I mused on the story. "A remarkable career has he. From Royalist officer, to condemned prisoner, to wanted fugitive, to drunken doctor, to suicidal gambler, to parson of the local church. That's rather an unlikely vocational pathway, is it not?"

"Is it?" John glanced at me, then continued. "I go often to discourse with Holy Mr. Gifford. At times I come away greatly comforted; at other times I come away worse and worse, my sins and troubles overwhelming me, laying me as low as hell."

Little did John or I know how overwhelmed with troubles he was about to be.

22

Unpardonable Sinner

That same night, the bells tolled from the ancient bell tower. Long and mournful, echoing along the humble cottages that lined the High Street. There was no merriment in their ringing that night. I dreaded what misery they heralded to our little village.

I momentarily cheered myself with the thought that it could be the old John Bunyan at another of his pranks, ringing the bells, sending the signal to the community that someone had died, when they hadn't; surely it would merely be more of his tomfoolery. It was only a fleeting hope, however, for I knew that John had sworn off ringing the bells, too fearful was he that the steeple itself might topple and crush him. No, it would not be John ringing those bells.

At first light I learned the unhappy news. John Bunyan's beloved wife—the delivering up of their last child had proven too much for her. She had expired in the night, leaving him widower with four young children, the eldest one blind as a fruit bat.

These were somber days in Elstow and Bedford. Poor as John Bunyan was, there was little time for grieving. If he did not labor at his tinker trade, his children would not eat. But to fulfill his calling, he was forced to leave them in the care of their elder sister, who, for all her tender heart and good intentions, was blind and little able to care for her younger siblings.

Meanwhile, I observed the terror in his countenance, the darting eyes, his pallid features, the hunched shoulders, his terrified glancing from side to side, and ever upward, as if he feared yet another blow about to descend upon him.

I drew near him to offer what words of consolation I might manage to cobble together for his comfort.

"Harry," said he, eyes as baleful as a cornered stag. "A very great storm has come upon me. Comfort is taken from me. Darkness has seized upon me. Floods of blasphemies against God, Christ, and the Scriptures are poured upon my spirit, to my great confusion."

I stammered, groping for words, my mouth opening and closing. I must have looked like a codfish. Words utterly failed me; try as I might, none came. So, I remained dumb, though my mouth gaped in astonishment at the virulence of his grief.

"This is all my doing," said he, both his hands clenched in a fistful of his rusty hair, his body rocking side to side with each word. "My dear wife's taking off, it is God's just judgment upon me for my blasphemies.

"You know me, Harry, better than any man. You know what I say is true. I deserve this at his hands. But why must my wife suffer, and now my children suffer without their dear mother? Why, Harry? It is *my* sin, *my* blasphemy. Why cannot it by *my alone* condemnation and suffering? Why must others suffer for *my* sins?"

He paused for breath. I felt, of all men, most inadequate to attempt an answer to his logorrhea. Yet, he pressed on.

"I have found in my mind a sudden urge to curse and swear, to speak some grievous thing against God. Surely, Harry, I am possessed of the devil. Horrible blasphemies do bolt out of my heart against God."

He broke off, his jaw set, his eyes flashing fire at the gray heavens above us. I worried that his grief had made him bereft of his senses.

"Oh, these are most tormenting cogitations," said he. "Harry, give me comfort."

Haltingly, I suggested that perhaps he ought to go see this Mr. Gifford of whom he spoke, the blasphemer-turned-parson. Yet did I fear sending him on his own in such a state. What if he were to do himself a harm in the river?

23

Thousand Gallons of Blood

In the weeks ahead, I did chance to cross paths from time to time with John Bunyan. Elstow and Bedford—ours was a small, close-knit community. It was impossible not to.

On one such occasion, I overtook John in Bedford along the towpath south of the river, its dark waters babbling their way to the far-off North Sea, ducks and coots plying the waters, bobbing for their breakfast. Above all, the grand spire of St. Paul's church pointed heavenward over the town, as it had done for centuries.

On that early autumn morning, I surveyed the village coming to life all about us. A farmer with his ox cart full of cabbages crossing the bridge, his ox's hooves clopping and the cartwheels clattering on the paving stones; children laughing and splashing in the river alongside where their mothers pounded out the laundry; a merchant standing precariously on a stool as he unfurled an awning over where he would sell his wares at the market that day; a black and tan dog barking and frolicking with the children in the shallows; the local earl wearing blue silk culottes, bestride a finely groomed mare, lace fluttering in the morning breeze from the man's sleeves.

John and I had halted at the place where the ancients used to ford the river, hence, the name Bedford. It was now spanned by a medieval bridge, as it had been for centuries. But it was more than a bridge, more than merely a means of crossing the river without getting one's feet wet. Generations before, a long-dead mayor had commissioned the construction of the town jail in a stone tower at the midspan, another tower added later to make room for more prisoners.

In a flurry of beating wings, a pigeon darted from under one of the stone arches of the bridge, and then another followed. From where we had halted, I could just make out the crisscrossing of iron bars on the small openings that served as windows in the tower jail at the midspan of the bridge.

After we had greeted one another and commented on the beauty of the morning, I made to inquire about his wellbeing. "How are you coping, John?" I stammered, not being a man of eloquence.

He thanked me very kindly for sending him to speak with the parson John Gifford, gesturing with a thumb over his shoulder back toward St. John's chapel, and told me he was somewhat better. I assured him that somewhat better was a good thing, and I was much relieved to hear of it.

"I do find myself, as it were," said he, "at times bemired in a bog, more loathsome in my own eyes than... than one of those." His anvil balanced on his shoulder, he gestured with his elbow at a toad crouching in the mud along the banks of the river, its wide throat heaving and pulsing, its eyes staring warily at us.

Hoping for levity to ease the moment, I assured him that I had only rarely thought of him as looking over-much like a toad inhabiting a miry bog. By his reaction, I am uncertain if the attempted jest was well placed.

"Just when I think I have found a shred of hope to cling to," he continued, "God's just judgment of me strikes my conscience once again like a thunderbolt, and my twisting, and languishing, and pining away under the mighty hand of God return. I feel my very body trembling, and my whole mind shaking and tottering under his dreadful judgment. I feel also such a clogging and heat at my stomach, by reason of my terror, that I feel as if my breastbone would split asunder."

I stared at him, wide-eyed, like the toad.

"Harry, at times I fear that mine is the same fate as Judas's, that I too will fall headlong and burst asunder, and all my bowels will gush out."

Spellbound by his words, I was alarmed, and felt a rising dread in my own soul.

"At times such as these, Harry, I feel so heavy a load of guilt that I do twist and shrink under the burden thereof, a burden that so oppresses me that I can neither stand nor go, nor lie at rest."

He paused for breath, his brow furrowed, his eyes following the flight of a lone raven searching for carrion along the banks of the river.

"I have found my unbelief," he continued, "to set as it were my shoulder to the door to keep God out, even as part of my heart cries out, 'Good Lord, break it open. Lord, break these gates of brass, and cut these bars of iron.'

"I do feel as if I were in a dungeon, a man, as it were, locked up in an iron cage, as if I were the foulest of criminals bound in chains and in miseries." His eyes locked on the towers of the jail, he visibly shuddered. "I feel that it was me held forever just there in our Bedford jail. You know me, Harry, I could never bear that. Yet do I know that I deserve it. At times I feel that none but the devil himself can equal me for inward wickedness and pollution of mind."

Running his fingers through his hair, he broke off, a tremor appearing to pass through his entire body.

"And you describe this," said I, haltingly, "as doing somewhat better?"

A fortnight later, as I made my way in my best clothes for Bedford, and to what I hoped would be my new calling, just rounding a turn in the highway, I was suddenly arrested by what I saw.

There was John Bunyan, the burdens of his trade carelessly set aside, gazing out over a newly plowed field, as if it were heaven itself. There was not another living soul moving about on the road. Perplexed, I followed his gaze.

At the far edge of the field there was the farmer just visible unharnessing his team of draft horses and leading them to the barn for their mash and rub down after a long day of labor in that field. I knew having been raised by my farmer father, that it was plowed for the planting of winter wheat, the specifics of which may not be important, so I shall return to my narrative.

As so often happens during and after plowing, birds gather over the newly turned clods of earth, therein to feast on worms and other earth-dwelling larvae exposed by the turning of the soil.

So distracted was John Bunyan, that he had not observed my approach. Hence, with stealth, I stepped off the road, through the ditch, and over the dyke. Concealed thereby, on the opposite side of the dyke from he, I drew closer to observe him.

It was then that I saw them; three or four crows had descended onto the plowed earth, the late afternoon sunlight glistening deep blue on their plumage. And there was John gazing in wonder at them, or was it something else? And then I heard his voice. I was bewildered. Was the man speaking, engaged in familiar conversation with crows?

John Bunyan was not like other men; of that I had long been convinced. But for equally as long, since our boyhood, I had had this nagging fear. Was he simply a man with an over-fulminating imagination, or was he stark raving mad? While engaged in these troubling reflections, concealed behind the dyke, I was now sufficiently close to hear his words.

"'You are my love; you are my love.'"

Those were his words, verbatim, and he said them for emphasis many times over. My anxieties seemingly confirmed, I feared he had become strangely bewitched by the crows themselves. But then he continued.

"I had long felt like the demon-possessed child brought to Christ, thrown down by the devil, rent and tormented by the fiend as I wallowed on the ground, foaming at the mouth. That was me. And then I feared the day of grace was passed, and I was forever a castaway. And deserved to be so. Blasphemer that I was, my sins were unpardonable. There was no amount of grace sufficient to cover my foulness. There was no electing love sufficient for so wicked a man as I knew myself to have been."

I sat aghast at what I heard and saw that day. But as John spoke thus to the birds, more gathered. Drawn by the pungent aroma of newly plowed ground, a murder of crows descended, scolding and cawing, joining their fellows in the evening meal.

Suddenly, I felt the accelerations of amusement rising in my gorge. John Bunyan was ever the gatherer, had been so since our youth. And here was he gathering crows out in a field, so as it appeared, to preach to them. He continued his exhortation.

"Just when I was at my wit's ends, it was then when I read the words, 'You are my love.' 'You are my love, and nothing shall separate you from my love.' Then further, guided by divine grace, I read the words, 'My grace is sufficient for thee.' At this reassurance, I could not tell how to contain myself till I got to my home. '*Sufficient for thee*'!"

He broke off, so moved by his own sermon, for the instant, unable to continue.

"I saw with the eyes of my soul," said he, when he found his voice, "Jesus Christ at God's right hand. I saw that it was not my good frame of heart that made my righteousness better, nor yet my bad frame that made my righteousness worse. My righteousness is Jesus Christ himself, 'the same yesterday, today, and forever.' Christ is all—all my righteousness, all my sanctification, and all my redemption. And Christ and I are one. His righteousness mine, his merits mine, his victory also mine. Oh, Christ, Christ! There is nothing but Christ who is before my eyes."

Another murder of crows circled overhead, then descended upon the field as he spoke these words.

"Now have my chains fallen off my legs, and I am loosed from my afflictions and irons. Oh, had I a thousand gallons of blood within my veins," he continued, his voice low with emotion and resolve, "I could freely spill it all at the command and feet of this my Lord and Savior."

In wonder, I held my breath at his words, crouched in my concealment by the dyke, my legs prickling and tingling.

I heard John indrawing his breath and then easing it out in a sigh, now no longer of despair but of settled contentment. Lingering, he began humming a tune, one I had never heard before. He seemed in no hurry to gather his tools and be on his way.

Meanwhile, I was nearly at my wit's end. I had not planned how to extricate myself from my posture of spying, and wondered how much longer I could crouch in such a position before my legs would altogether lose any sense of feeling and give way beneath me.

John drew in another great breath, and then spoke once again. "Come forth, Harry. You must be in great discomfiture squatting there for so long behind the dyke. Walk with me on the highway."

24

Mending Souls

Mortified at my abortive attempt at spying, when I had recovered myself, I staggered from behind the dyke and joined him as he requested.

That evening stroll with John Bunyan along the highway—the King's Highway, as he called it—began the first planting of the seeds of doubt in my breast. But I hastily pushed those doubts aside. I refused to believe any of it.

Men do not change. Leastwise, a man like I knew John Bunyan to be. But his impassioned words to me that evening of a new birth, of a new beginning, of a new life, "Life! Life! Eternal life!" he called it, began planting a new seed, but it was a very small seed, and my rocky soil would prove most barren, as events would demonstrate in the days ahead.

In these very days, changes were afoot for the likes of Harry Wylie. It was inviably believed by our feudal landlords in times past, that once a landless farmer's son, as I had been, always a landless farmer's son. But times were changing. My father's landlord was brother-in-law to the magistrate in Bedford, from whom we learned that there was a new vocation for me, if I would have it, and if the council would have me. Opportunity had come knocking at my door. I was being elevated, a man climbing the pinnacle of respectable society.

In brief, I was being made jailer at the town jail, midspan on the Bedford bridge, with duties that extended to the county jail on the corner of Silver Street and High Street. With my elevation, the world lay at my feet, as I believed it to be so. New-found wealth lay all about me. I took up residence in a stone cottage provided by the town council hard by the bridge so as to be near my responsibilities, the town jail never far from my line of sight.

Not certain how I was to go about disposing of all the pound sterling that made up my salary and the measure of grain, beef, and beer that came with the new vocation, I cast about looking for a woman. After all, it was only fitting that a man in my exalted station in life should take a wife. And so, thusly, I did.

Meanwhile, my new vocation gave me ample opportunity to observe John as he plied his craft with augmented zeal, but it was no longer a single craft. His was a dual calling, so he seemed to feel it, as evidenced by his practice of his callings. Wandering the countryside with the burdens of his tinker trade

154

upon his shoulders, John made not only to mend pots and kettles, but to mend human souls—or so it appeared.

"Pots to mend, knives to grind—any work for a tinker?" It was the same wherever I happened to hear him herald his trade. Crowds gathered to John like hummingbirds to nectar. It was always so wherever I chanced to come across the man: throughout Bedfordshire, and beyond, wherever he was to wander—Stevington, Harlington, Lower Samsell, Eaton Socon, Ampthill, Olney, even far-off Cambridge—wherever he roamed.

He had learned his tinker craft from his father's vocation, but he explained to me that he was learning his itinerant preaching craft from Holy Mr. Gifford.

"Aha, the gambling parson his own self," I taunted.

"As *was*," said he, emphasizing the past tense. "Under the ministry of Holy Mr. Gifford, how my soul has been led on from truth to truth! As I hear his words, methinks I have seen the Christ born; it is as if I have seen him grow up, as if I had seen him walk through this world from his cradle to his cross, seen how gently he gave himself to be hanged and nailed upon it for my sins and my wicked doings. And, as I muse on Christ's progress, Mr. Gifford reminds me that Scripture says Christ Jesus was ordained for the slaughter. Harry, there has not been one part of the gospel of the Lord Jesus but by Mr. Gifford I have been convincingly led into it."

He then proceeded to tell me of another man, an associate of Gifford's, a young man by the name of John Burton. Hereafter, I frequently saw the two Johns plying the countryside for converts, taking turns preaching in the fields, barns, public squares, medieval crosses, wherever they chanced to gather a crowd.

Cynic that I had become, I was often torn asunder by these developments. I felt I knew John Bunyan's heart. This his preaching stage was merely a fad, another outward episode of sham reformation. I rehearsed the sins of our youth in my memory. After all we had experienced together, I was more than ever convinced that hobgoblins remain hobgoblins, that leopards do not change their spots, and madmen do not change from their insanity. John Bunyan himself had forced me to these conclusions.

I was convinced that all of his new preaching and piety was just him putting on respectability as one puts on a new waistcoat. That was all. John saw herein a new opportunity for gathering, for entertaining the masses. He had observed which way the wind was blowing. Profanity had fallen out of fashion; piety was very much in the popular way in Puritan England. What better way than to assume the role of a man who weekly steps into the high pulpit, there to entertain his hearers, to amuse them, to gather more acclaim for himself.

I knew John Bunyan by the back. This was merely a new stage on which he would be the principal player, the only player. So, I had convinced myself to believe.

And then early one morning in September 1655, I awoke with a start. It was the ominous tolling of the bells of St. Paul's in Bedford that had awakened me. I soon learned that the only man who had managed to settle the troubled brains of John Bunyan, Holy

156

Mr. Gifford, had expired suddenly in the night. The gambling parson was dead. Recalling the dark valley through which Bunyan passed upon his wife's death, I feared for how the news would fall upon him.

25

Prating Coxcomb

Bedford is a small town, and in the days that followed, news travelled fast. The congregation meeting at St. John's parish church just south of the river, now bereft of their beloved pastor, called young John Burton to take up the sacred responsibility.

It chanced that young Burton had been granted the privilege of academic learning; though, I am told, he never scorned to be seen with rustic John Bunyan despite the man's complete absence thereof. Different though these two Johns were, their combined gifts drew ever larger crowds to hear their preaching.

Whether at the parish church in Bedford, its medieval nave packed shoulder-to-shoulder on the Sabbath Day, or amongst the ditches and hedgerows of the surrounding shires, vast crowds would gather to hear the young scholar and the ignorant tinker. Much to my astonished bewilderment, I saw it on numerous occasions with my own eyes, and heard it with my own ears.

One such occasion was when my vocation took me some miles away to Cambridge. Amongst the exalted spires of the ancient university city, its cobbled streets filled with capped and gowned scholars, all speaking Latin, there was John Bunyan in coarse homespun garments, shod with much-worn, and out of fashion, bucket-top boots, his anvil upon one shoulder and his tinker tools slung upon the other.

Walking down King's Parade at Bunyan's side, John Burton blended in more naturally with the exalted architecture and company. But I believe there was never a greater disjoining of persons than the learned scholar ambling alongside a laboring man such as Bunyan carrying his burden down the illustrious corridors of learning in that city.

From where I lurked across the street, in the shadows of the porter house of King's College, I watched as John, with an effortless heave, hoisted his anvil off his shoulder and into the turf on the north side of the west entrance to Great St. Mary's Church, right next to the booth of a vendor hawking fresh roasted chestnuts. I knew it to be so, for the breeze carried the nutty richness of their roasting to my nostrils, setting my stomach to growling for my luncheon.

And then he did it. "Kettles to mend, knives to sharpen—any work for the tinker?"

I knew what he was scheming, and wondered at his brazen manner of going about it. Had he no sense of self-respect, of what is fitting in such a place? I wanted to bury my face in shame at him.

Tugging at the back of my brain was the affront that John and his preaching were to my theory. I kept telling myself that he did it for acclaim, to attract attention to himself, to take center stage, as it were. Yet, did I know, deep down, that if it were true, no sane man would go about seeking greatness for himself by John Bunyan's method. He might seek disdain and derision, thereby, but not greatness.

A man who sought the esteem of the learned world would never strap on his work-worn apron and his ridiculous one-legged stool in the magnificent shadow of King's College Chapel, its stained glass sparkling in the midday sun, its Gothic arches rising into the blue heavens. No self-respecting man would fire up his brazier, and begin tap-tapping with his infernal hammers on his blasted anvil in so grand a setting.

But I knew what was coming. Shameless, unadorned preaching, and with that preaching the crowds would gather like a murder of crows dropping from the sky onto a dead cat.

Riveting a new handle on a kettle for her, John chatted merrily with the stout middle-aged woman roasting and selling the chestnuts. As Bunyan chitchatted and worked, directly above him the bells of the university church began their hourly ringing. As their gonging echoed off the honey-colored stone edifices lining the street, John paused in his labors.

Then, I watched him look slowly upward, his eyes following the stone tracery in the Gothic arched windows of Great St. Mary's, and farther upward to the four castle-like turrets at the very top of the bell tower.

That infernal daydreaming look came into his eyes, and a smile played at the corners of his mouth, as if he was recalling a private jest. Gone was any sign of discomfiture. He sat at his ease at the foot of a bell tower standing more than 100 feet directly above his head. I could not explain how it was that all of his former terror of the bells and the tower falling and crushing him under their weight was now gone forever, so it seemed.

In spite of my embarrassment at the man, I crossed the King's Parade and drew near. Though I was ashamed even to acknowledge that I knew the man, I somehow felt compelled to draw near. As black-gowned scholars passed by, their robes swishing 'round their ankles, leather tomes under their arms, engaged in eloquent discourse in Latin, I felt my neck and face grow hot with humiliation.

Here sat a man with no more formal education than he and I had managed to acquire at Harpur Grammar School in our youth, and as I came within earshot I could tell by that fire in his eyes and the eager glow on his features that he had already shifted from friendly conversation about the weather, the chestnuts, the beauty, the birds, the architecture. Surrounded by the greatest men of learning in the realm, the tinker from nowhere had commenced his sermon. No sane man would attempt it, and I mused upon the extent of his madness; surely, it was incurable.

"There is no good in this life but what is mingled with some evil," he was saying as I came closer still. Others by this time had gathered, jostling and pressing in all about him. I noticed that some of the aspiring scholars, little more than boys, were winking at each other. I caught sight of one rascal attempting to conceal a basket of some species of fruit or vegetable in the folds of his black gown. I groaned inwardly. It was not a good portent for the one delivering the sermon.

"Honors perplex, riches disquiet, and pleasures ruin health. But in heaven we shall find blessings in their purity, without any ingredient to embitter, with everything to sweeten them.

"Oh! Who is able to conceive the inexpressible, inconceivable joys that are there? None but they who have tasted of them. Lord, help us to put such a value upon them here, that in order to prepare ourselves for them, we may be willing to forego the loss of all the deluding pleasures here."

From the shadows where I attempted to hide myself in the press of the crowd, I failed to see the hurling of the first missile. It landed with a *Splat!* To his credit, the young lout had a good arm, good arm and eye. The mushy interior of a fully ripe tomato burst like a wound directly on John Bunyan's forehead.

There was a sharp intaking of breath from the crowd, and then uproarious laughter from the young scholar and his followers, hilarity that tittered to some of the other onlookers.

I knew the combustible character of John's temper in our youth, and worried that he would irreparably discredit himself by discharging a torrent of cursing. I had heard him erupt in a proliferation of profanity for far less aggravation many times before. A great deal depended on the next few seconds of his life, I was certain, and observed his reaction closely.

Crossing his eyes, John made as if to look upward at the exploded remains of tomato dripping from his brow. With a good-humored laugh, he wiped away the glob with his sleeve. Then, as if nothing had occurred, he simply resumed his discourse.

"Christ is the desire of nations, the joy of angels, the delight of the Father; with what solace then must that soul be filled that hath the possession of him to all eternity?

"Oh! What acclamations of joy will there be when all the children of God shall meet together, without fear!"

Extending his calloused hands toward the crowd as a father might invite his children into his embrace, John continued.

"Is there not a time coming when the godly may ask the wicked what profit they have in their pleasure? What comfort in their greatness? And what satisfaction in all their labor and learning?"

His discourse at an end, John wiped his brow a second time, and set a small cast-iron pan of solder to melt over his brazier.

"Prating coxcomb!" The scornful words emanated from a pompous and professorial sounding voice.

"The words of the esteemed Thomas Smith," murmured a fellow at my elbow, pressing in close to me. "Professor of Arabic, is he, and keeper of the university library." He nodded sagely at his own words.

"Hear, hear!" several voices agreed.

"Who authorized a gibbering tinker to preach such putrefaction in our streets?"

"My esteemed colleague," interjected another sophisticated voice. "You seem to be angry with the tinker because he strives to mend souls, as well as kettles and pans. Whilst I have often sat in bewildered wonder at your erudite expostulations, and am wholly unmoved by the same. By this man's mastery of unadorned Anglo-Saxon English, and his prodigious knowledge of Holy Scripture, the tinker proves his mission and commission from the church and congregation in Bedford."

The man at my elbow explained: "The words of the esteemed William Dell, Master of Caius College, just there." He nodded down the street toward the porter house of the college.

"The proof of the tinker's commission," agreed another, "does very much seem to be in the pudding."

And then I heard another voice from the back of the crowd, a soft, almost feeble voice, one I knew I had heard before.

"This man is not chosen out of an earthly, but out of the heavenly university."

"And just what university might that be?" retorted Thomas Smith.

"The Church of Jesus Christ. It appears to me, that the tinker hath, through grace, taken these three heavenly degrees: to wit, union with Christ, the anointing of the Spirit, and the experience of the temptation of Satan, which do more fit a man for that mighty work of preaching the gospel than all university learning and degrees that can be had."

"Who, pray tell, is that man?" It was the fellow tugging at my elbow posing the question.

Pleased at myself for knowing the answer, I leaned close and cupped my hand around his ear. "It is the scholar, John Burton, parson of St. John's parish church in Bedford."

As the crowds dispersed—some, to be sure, scoffing and rolling their eyes in condescension—I watched in wonder as Dr. William Dell and several other men, wearing the exalted garments of learning, approached John Bunyan, readily clasping his work-soiled hands and thanking him for his apt words. Here was the lowly tinker alongside men of the greatest learning in the realm. I suspect that my mouth hung agape; for, of a certainty, I was all astonishment at the sight.

I would, however, observe similar encounters in the future, and was forced to conclude that John Bunyan seemed never intimidated by or ashamed before the giants of learning and academia.

Unlike almost all other men, much to my bewilderment, the lowly tinker neither despised the learned for their learning, nor fawned upon them for it either.

26

Change and Decay

On the street in Cambridge, I described John Burton's voice as feeble, for so it was. And so was the man. Feeble men often die young, and so John Burton was taken off several months later in 1656, leaving the congregation of St. John's parish church, once again, without a parson and preacher.

I feared how, yet again, passing through the shadow of the valley of death might trouble the brains of John Bunyan and return him to his former disquiet. I need not have worried. He grieved, as other men do, but without despair, as he had so done at the all-too recent passing of Holy Mr. Gifford (I shall discontinue referring to him as the gambling parson; for, I am told, it is unwise to speak ill of the dead).

Meanwhile, the inexplicable phenomenon continued. High and low clamored by the hundreds to hear the tinker preach, and that from all parts of middle England. Some, to be sure, to mock—but many more to marvel—at his words. As his notoriety increased, some of the more skeptical clergy felt compelled, however reluctantly, to open their pulpits to the tinker.

In my elevated station in society it seemed more fitting that I and my new wife attend divine services, not at the diminutive parish church on the south side of the river, but at the grand cathedral-like church of St. Paul's in the center square of Bedford town, a location with an illustrious history dating back to the year of our Lord 800 when an Anglo-Saxon missionary founded a church here in what was then called Beda's ford.

The Sabbath morning of May 23, 1656, began like any other, my wife dutifully upon my arm, as we strolled across the bridge, along the embankment, past the Swan Inn, and into St. Paul's Square, bells summoning us to worship from the medieval spire rising high above the town.

It was a lovely spring morning, the square decorated with lavender, yellow, white, and blue sweet pea blossoms, the air scented with the delicious orangey flavors of the first blooms of the syringa bush encircling the flagstones of the square.

Once inside the nave, I escorted my wife to our sitting place, for in my station in the community, I was granted exclusive use of and perpetual seating in our own space, as is fitting. Once ensconced in our proper place, I gazed up at the 13th century arches lining the nave, and upward to the delicately carved, oak ceiling high above us, composing my mind for the duty before us by meditating upon the prodigious labors of the medieval craftsmen, and the permanence and beauty of the work of their hands.

Imagine my astonishment on that Sabbath morning of May 23, 1656, when none other than John Bunyan mounted the spiraling staircase to the pulpit and presumed to preach from so illustrious a situation. In his plain tunic and dull waistcoat and britches of charcoal gray, he seemed so very out of place in the splendors of that pulpit.

I recall only snippets of his preaching that morning: "If you would have life, eternal life, you must fly from the wrath to come!"

Slouching in my chair, I folded my arms across my chest. I was perfectly content to remain on cordial terms with Bunyan as long as he remained within the confines of his calling. The man was a laborer; a tinker, and a common tinker he must remain, so I strongly felt. His being up there was beneath the dignity of the place, and I felt out of sorts at his intrusion. Clearly the vicar must have invited him, though, no doubt, under duress. I felt certain he was preaching directly to me, and had a vague sense of having heard some of it before.

"Will you leave your sins and go to heaven," he cried, at one point in his exhortation, "or have your sins and go to hell?"

Imagine my further astonishment more than half a year later when news spread throughout the town that the congregation of St. John's parish church, "after prayerful consideration," called none other than the tinker to be their pastor. Times must have become desperate, indeed, in that little place, south of the river.

At the supper table, over beef and ale pie, I assured my wife that I knew the man by the back, inside and outside the man. And I allowed myself to make a mocking jest of the notion of one with such a history as John Bunyan being fit to attend to the spiritual needs of anyone—anyone besides crows and puddles.

It was uncanny how our lives, John Bunyan's and mine, almost as if by some divine decree, intertwined with one another.

About this same time, as I had done, he too took a wife, another woman, and, with his new wife and his four children by his previous wife, he now resided at a small cottage on St. Cuthbert's Street in Bedford. When first he had taken up residence here it was to be nearer to Holy Mr. Gifford and to carry on his tinker trade in the larger of the two villages. Yet, first Gifford and then Burton, now gone, and here John Bunyan was, fully ensconced in my town.

Elizabeth Bunyan proved to be an extraordinarily remarkable specimen of a woman, as imminently forthcoming events would demonstrate her great need of so being.

How a new wife can take up the duties of caring for the children of another woman with the doting tenderness that Elizabeth did is beyond me. There was nothing of the proverbial evil stepmother in Bunyan's new wife Elizabeth. Her selfless devotion to her husband and her tireless attention to the needs of his children defied human categories, but was, for all of that, the more spoken of in the community.

For his part, John was ever taking her arm, doting on her as if his peasant wife were a princess, and he did it all in public and in a most shameless fashion.

Meanwhile, news arrived from London. Oliver Cromwell, Lord Protector of England, had fallen gravely ill. It was speculated that the untimely death of his daughter only a month before had made him the more vulnerable to the tertian ague that had set upon him. Fearing the worst, Cromwell made it official: he appointed his son Richard as his successor. On September 3, 1658, at Whitehall, the great military commander breathed his last. With all solemn rites and ceremony, the remains of the Lord Protector of England were laid to rest in Westminster Abbey.

27

Sins of Our Youth

Oliver Cromwell—dead. Old Ironsides himself, the creator of the New Model Army. Dead.

There was talk of little else. Speculation and fear reigned in the bosom of many. What would it mean for England? Parliament under Oliver Cromwell's leadership had committed regicide, beheaded their king. A king who had a son. A son of the same name who intended, so it was rumored throughout the realm, to return and take up what was rightfully his, the throne. A restored monarchy. But what would such a restoration mean for the Puritans and for the church?

Idle speculation, I was to learn, did little to alter my duties. Prison was prison, and chains were chains, and prisoners were prisoners. My duties were little changed by political upheaval, or so I supposed at the time.

One day as I rode my mare—for, in my dignified profession, I was deemed worthy of riding about the countryside rather than walking—as I say, I was riding my horse along Silver Street in Bedford, after having just transferred a prisoner from the town jail on the bridge to the county jail, when, lo and behold, there was John Bunyan, his brazier glowing hot, the smoke rising at his side.

Placing a gloved hand upon my hip, I looked down at him from where I sat high atop my steed. I felt an uncontrollable urge to mock him. Parson though he was, yet here he was still tapping away with his little hammers at his meagre trade.

A crowd had gathered; more than two dozen folk surrounded the man. I was certain they could not all be there with their crook pots needing his tinkering, but there they were; drawn by, if by nothing else, his wit and charming ways. Just as I made to spur my horse onward on my errand, my attention was arrested by his words.

He was speaking as if in some kind of confession. "...I was and have been polluted, very much polluted with original corruption. For, to speak my mind freely, I do confess, that it is mine opinion, that children come polluted with sin into the world, and oft-times the sins of our youth are indulged upon more by virtue of indwelling sin than by sinful examples that are set before them by others. The root of sin lies within, for from within the heart of man proceedeth sin."

The sins of our youth. I had heard enough and spurred my horse onward, my mind awhirl with memories.

172

I had heard the newly improved John Bunyan lament the hobgoblins of his youth; and, God and I know, there were sins aplenty for which he very much needed an eloquent canticle of lamentation, mournfully sung by a vast melodious host.

I had long thought myself safely in the shadow of his immense repository of transgressions, securely to leeward of his heavily laden barquentine of iniquities. Looking back upon our misspent youth, I believe I had come to depend on his greater badness as a bulwark to my own. Surely God would not strike so mediocre a sinner such as I, when the paragon of profanity himself lay readily to hand, head and shoulders above the rest. So, I had reasoned, wittingly or unwittingly, until one night early in the year 1658.

Celebrating the second anniversary of my elevation in society—I am forced to confess it—I drank too much ale. As near as I am able or care to remember, one of my prison associates urged me into it, to retell stories of the sins of my youth. The more I told, the more I found it impossible to separate the sins of my youth from the far greater transgressions of John Bunyan's youth. Basking in the obsequious attentions of my colleagues, and lubricated by the ale, my tongue began wagging outside of all boundaries. I told of his mad antics, his blasphemies, his profane poetry, his iniquitous songs.

More ale, more egging on by my punitive associates.

"A man bewitched is he," said I.

"Bewitched, did you say?" slurred one of my attendees. "Be-witched, be he a witch, then?"

"A witch, a Jesuit, a highwayman," said I, holding my pint in the air. "Ah, and far worse. Does anyone of us

173

think that an itinerant laboring man, moving freely about the countryside, unchaperoned, caring for the domestic needs of the kitchen and of those who dwell therein, ever consorting with the fairer sex, does anyone of us deny that the man keeps a mistress— nay, no doubt, keeps several mistresses?"

More ale. More raucous laughter at my speculative telling. "And I have heard it on good authority that the man has two wives at one and the same time, like a heathen."

"How is it," asked one of my listeners, smothering a belch into his sleeve, "that such a reprobate as he has now become the town preacher?"

"*Unauthorized* preacher," I corrected him, clonking my mug onto the ale bench for emphasis.

When I came more to my sense, my head pounding as if an anvil had fallen upon it, I felt shame at all I had said that night. But when I made an attempt to discredit my own talebearing, my new friends would hear none of it. There was far too much pleasure to be had in believing such things of the newly improved John Bunyan to quibble over-much about the veracity of the details.

Imagine my humiliation, when several weeks later at an inquest in Eaton Socon, John Bunyan was called to answer charges that had been levelled against him, charges that sounded more than vaguely similar to my drunken talebearing, everything from the ridiculous notion that he was a witch to the entirely accurate charge of his unauthorized preaching. I knew the rest all to be falsehoods, absurd fabrications of the inebriate's tongue, of my tongue. I cast about for a way to make things right, but I was to discover that it was as easy to take back falsehoods as it was to restrain yesterday's tide.

When called to testify against him before the magistrate at Eaton Socon, I denied being of sound mind when I said any of it, and that none of it was true. Somehow, I managed to persuade the magistrate, and keep John Bunyan, and myself, out of the clink. All charges were dropped; but, in the months ahead, I was to learn that slanderous memories, however wildly false, by malicious minds are never entirely forgotten.

28

Bunyan Oak

I was to learn that my exalted new vocation ever bound me up with magistrates, trials, chains, and prisoners. As was the case when, on a day, I was commissioned to retrieve a man arrested, tried, and convicted by a local magistrate hard by Lower Samsell, several miles south of Bedford. I was ordered to transport the prisoner, bound in chains, to the county jail in Bedford. It was whilst fulfilling my commission that I next saw and heard John Bunyan.

It was but a week after my return from denying the charges against him before the magistrate in Eaton Socon. I felt humiliated by my indiscretion and had hoped to avoid seeing him for far longer than a mere week. But as I rode my mare along Harlington Road, in the countryside by the hamlet of Lower Samsell, my attention was arrested by a gathering of rural folks, farmers and the like. They swelled from the hillsides like waves of the sea. It was no small gathering, and I wondered if there was to be a market or a fair, though I had never heard of one in that place. I should have known the cause.

Waving and greeting folks, many by name, there was John Bunyan in the center of the gathering. I recognized the eight-year-old girl at his side, her bonnet pulled back, and her auburn curls tumbling riotously about her slender shoulders. It was his blind daughter Mary, was she, never far from his protective reach.

I reined in my horse. Though I had seen these Bunyan gatherings before, common as they were becoming, it never ceased to amaze me seeing such a scene unfolding before my eyes. Though it was far from any village or hamlet, and thus, far from those who would be drawn for his services in the mending of their pots and pans, yet here was a large gathering of people. I do not exaggerate to say there were a hundred, likely many more.

Inconvenient for his trade though it was, John could not have chosen a more picturesque location. I dismounted my beast and freed her to graze on the lush, spring grass surrounding the tree. The massive arboreal specimen stood atop a hillside, a flock of sheep grazing below in a fertile basin, rimmed in the far distance by a jagged escarpment, the meadow encircled more closely by rolling hillsides checkered with a network of hawthorn hedges.

So vast was the trunk of the giant oak tree that I estimated six grown men could not span its base with their arms wide spread, making a circle around it with fingers touching one another. Where the trunks of four main branches joined into the foremost stalk of that magnificent tree, there was a natural hollow, with irregularities approaching the hollow that resembled the steps to mount a pulpit. John now proceeded to mount those steps and take his place in what seemed to be a purpose-grown, open-air podium, the crowds drawing in closer beneath the tree.

I shook my head in wonder and could not leave off smiling, whether of scorn or wonder, I never could be sure which it would be.

It was so very like John Bunyan, his imagination spurred on by the large crowd and the majestic tree, its vast canopy of leafy branches acting the role of vaulted splendors above him. Tenderly, he helped little Mary to find a comfortable depression below his pulpit where she sat, her sightless eyes and face lifted toward where she knew her father to be. After greeting the congregation, he led in a prayer, read a few verses from his Bible, and then commenced his exhortation.

"The gospel of grace and salvation is above all doctrines the most dangerous," he began, his voice carrying over the leaves rustling in the branches above him. His hearers grew more attentive and silent as they listened.

"The most dangerous, if it be received in word only by graceless men—if it be not attended with a sensible need of a Savior, and bring them to him. For such men as have only the notion of it, are of all men most miserable—for by reason of their knowing more than heathens, this only shall be their final portion, that they shall have greater stripes."

I was not much of a man for sermons in these days, and I was learning that John Bunyan's sermons always felt like he had custom crafted them for my ears. "Shall have greater stripes," is it? I glanced impatiently at my horse, hoping she would need attending to soon, thereby giving me a good excuse to be back on my way. While I cast about for a suitable distraction, John continued:

"As the devil labors by all means, as much as in him lies, to keep out other things that are good, so does he labor to keep out of thy heart the thoughts of passing from this life into another world; for he knows that if he can but keep thee from serious thoughts of death, he shall the more easily keep thee in thy sins.

"Nothing will make thee more earnest in working out thy salvation, than a frequent meditation upon thy mortality; nothing hath greater influence for taking off our hearts from vanities, and for the begetting in us desires after holiness than the contemplation of thy own dying.

"Oh sinner, what a condition wilt thou fall into when thou departest this world! If thou depart unconverted, thou hadst better have been smothered the first hour thou wast born; thou hadst better have been plucked one limb from another."

A black-and-white speckled rat terrier, so it appeared to be, suddenly rose up and began barking at John, its master reaching out to restrain the animal. I found the distraction welcome and humorous; but, looking about me, I must have been the only one.

"If thou depart unconverted," he continued, "thou hadst better have been made like this dog, or a toad, or a serpent, if thou die unconverted. Oh sinner, this thou wilt find true if thou repent not.

"When the sound of the trumpet shall be heard which shall summon the dead to appear before the tribunal of God, the righteous shall hasten out of their graves with joy to meet their Redeemer in the clouds; others shall call to these hills and mountains to fall upon them, to cover them from the sight of their Judge. Let thee therefore, in time, be posing to thyself the question: which of the two shall thou be?"

I both marveled and trembled at his words. There was no academic speculation in John Bunyan's preaching. I had on occasion heard that kind of pedantic parading of acumen in lectures by men from the highfalutin halls of learning. This was not that.

As John rounded to his conclusion, I looked to my horse, eager to be away. How could I face him after what I had done, what I had said in my inebriated condition, after the trouble I had caused him with the magistrate?

Just as I mounted my horse and was preparing to bury my heels into her flanks, John hailed me. For an instant, I considered ignoring him, pretending not to hear. But he was upon me, his hand stretched out toward my horse's reins, a disarming smile upon his ruddy features.

He greeted me. I could not look him in the eye, but stammered out what I hoped would be an adequate apology for my unintended libel.

"I bind these lies and slanders to me," said he, with a dismissive wave of his hand, "as an ornament. It belongs to my Christian profession to be vilified, slandered, reproached, and reviled. Harry, my good friend, I rejoice in reproaches for Christ's sake."

29

Damnable Traitors

T o say that I was dumbfounded at such a confession given to me by John Bunyan would be wholly inadequate to express my utter incredulity at his words. Rejoicing at being vilified, slandered, reproached, and reviled? What is wrong with a man who rejoices at such things?

In the course of time, and in the seeming happenstance of events, I came to be in a position to give John Bunyan a horse. Perhaps it was an act of penance on my part for my having so brutishly slandered him with my words. And I sincerely hoped that doing so balanced the scales in my favor.

It chanced that a man detained under my supervision for failing to pay his debts, had a horse confiscated by the magistrate. I say, a horse, but it was truly an ancient beast—once upon a time, no doubt, a fine draft horse, a laboring animal, a creature designed for bearing heavy burdens and lifting prodigious loads. But it appeared to be a sad and neglected horse, long since beyond its prime of life, so sorry a creature that none of the man's debtors would accept the animal in payment of his debts.

Being close to such proceedings as I was in my profession, I spoke up and acquired the ponderous old beast; and, not certain how long for this world he was, I hastily presented him as a gift to John Bunyan. Tramping around the countryside on his own two feet, the burdens of his trade weighing upon his shoulders, John could make good use of a horse, so I reasoned.

"He is a lovely creature, Harry," said John.

My face grew hot at his words, for I felt they were ironically exaggerated.

"Lovely, indeed. What is his name?"

"Uh, as far as the court knows, he is a horse without a name, none, that is, insofar as the record indicates. He is just a horse."

Murmuring softly to the beast, John stroked the large animal's velvety nose, and ran his hands over the sturdy neck and shoulders, its hide long neglected and in need of brushing and a good rub down.

"Mary, dear," said he to his daughter, heaving her up onto his shoulders so she could touch the beast. "What do you think we should call him?"

I watched as the blind lass ran her fingers over the horse's ears and through his coarse mane, her lips parted and wonder stretching across her sightless features. John walked slowly around the animal so she could thoroughly inspect him with her touch and with her nose. She used both hands to stroke his back and massive flanks.

"Well, dearest Mary, what do you think?"

"Can I sit upon him?" said she, her voice hushed with admiration.

Holding the halter, John leaned close to the animal's sides so she could climb up. Once on the horse's back, so wide was he, Mary's legs stuck almost straight out. Gently she took hold of a fistful of the horse's mane in each hand, laying her head alongside his neck.

"Deliverance," she whispered. "Father, is that a proper name for a horse, Deliverance?"

John smiled at me. "Harry, what do you think of such a name for a horse."

I mumbled that it was not my place to say, but it being their animal, they could name him whatsoever they fancied.

Thereafter, it became a common sight on the streets of Bedford and in the surrounding countryside to see John Bunyan and his daughter Mary being carried about by Deliverance. Under the doting ministrations of Mary, Deliverance's coat shimmered in the sunlight; his tail and mane were never matted and were often braided and decorated with colorful ribbons. More and more, Mary by herself could be seen either on the horse's broad back or walking along beside the great beast, she talking and laughing with Deliverance as if he understood and approved every word she said.

Meanwhile, tempestuous changes were afoot in the affairs of state. With the death of the Lord Protector, and the infighting of

Parliament and the army under the failing leadership of his son Richard Cromwell, rumblings arose from the Continent. Scheming in exile, Charles Stuart began courting Parliament for his restoration to the throne.

Puritan ministers feared the worst if the monarchy was restored to one such as Charles, known for his luxury-loving infidelities, and for his desire to restore the absolute power of the monarchy, so diminished when his father was defeated and beheaded by Parliament.

As a stratagem to allay such fears, Charles Stuart made extravagant promises. April 4, 1660, Charles issued the Declaration of Breda from his exile in the Netherlands. His words were much published abroad and hotly debated by Puritans throughout the realm.

"Because the uncharitableness of the times have produced several opinions in religion, by which men are engaged in animosities against each other, we do declare a liberty to tender consciences, and that no man shall be disquieted or called in question for differences of opinion in matters of religion, which do not disturb the peace of the kingdom; and that we shall be ready to consent to such an Act of Parliament, as, upon mature deliberation, shall be offered to us, for the full granting of that indulgence."

All of which sounded reassuring for those concerned about the free exercise of religious liberties in the realm, as his words were clearly intended to do. There was, however, considerable speculation about the meaning of "not disturbing the peace of the kingdom," and that bit about "upon mature deliberation." The aspiring monarch went on to declare amnesty for all who had taken up arms against the crown in the Civil War, a most-welcome provision for John and me, as we had done so, along with many others.

Determined to take possession of the right which he claimed God and Nature had made his due, conniving Charles II agreed to everything Parliament asked for, yet without legally obligating himself to do any of it, as events would prove.

Reassured by his promises, Parliament sent over the 80-gun ship of the line, *Naseby*, named for the decisive victory over Charles' father, the very one in which John and I had fought. Charles II promptly changed the vessel's name. He dubbed it *HMS Royal Charles* and then sailed for England to recover his throne and crown. Looking back, we all of us should have seen the royal vengeance coming.

Once in possession of his throne and crown, the new king wasted no time in restoring the exalted splendor of royalty. In his determination to rule by divine right, he wielded his scepter without restraint.

One of the new king's first commands was to have the body of Oliver Cromwell exhumed from his resting place in Westminster Abbey. After publicly beheading the corpse, he ordered the head to be spitted upon a pike over Westminster Hall, the very place Cromwell had held the trial of the new king's father Charles I in 1649, and from where the condemned monarch had been led to Whitehall and beheaded.

For the king's hedonistic indulgences and his profligate court full of drunkenness, promiscuity, and debauchery, his courtiers called Charles the "Merry Monarch." With Parliament now firmly controlled by his Royalist supporters, Charles saw to the passage of four statutes that would severally restrict freedom of religion for anyone who would not submit to fornicating Charles as the head of the church. One of those statutes strictly forbade unauthorized preaching without swearing an oath acknowledging the monarch's sole authority over the church.

Political unrest mounting, these were volatile and dangerous times for an unauthorized preacher like John Bunyan. But he seemed unruffled by the times and turned everything into a gospel metaphor, a sermon illustration, as it were. In the midst of these times when lesser men would keep their heads down, I overheard him preaching at St. Paul's Square, Bedford, a vast crowd pressing in about him. He sat bestride Deliverance, the horse I bequeathed to him now playing the role of four-legged pulpit for the man. Why had not I prescribed more restrictions on his use of the animal?

"There was a certain man that had committed treason against his king." I groaned at his opening remarks and buried my face in my hands. Did he not understand the times, that this was a most injudicious time for talking about treason to a king?

"But for as much as the king had compassion on him," he continued, "he sent him, by the hand of a faithful messenger, a pardon under his own hand and seal. But in the country where this poor man dwelt there were also many that sought to trouble him, by often putting him in mind of his treason, and the law that was to be executed on the offender.

"Now, how should this man honor his king? Surely, by believing the king's handwriting, which was his pardon! Certainly, he would honor him more by so doing, than to have regard to all the clamors of his enemies continually against him."

Confounded at his words, and fearing that John was about to commit the very treason of which he spoke, I shouldered my way closer, not certain what I was about to do, but hoping to stop his mouth, if I could. I scowled up at him, trying to get his attention, even flourishing my broad-brimmed hat at him.

"Just so it is here," he continued, avoiding my gesticulations and scowling eye. "Thou having committed treason against the King of heaven, he, through compassion for Christ's sake, hath sent thee a pardon. But the devil, the law, and thy conscience, do continually seek to disturb thee, by bringing thy sin afresh into thy remembrance.

"But now, wouldst thou honor thy King? Why, then, believe the record that God hath given of his Son. 'And this is the record, that God hath given to us eternal life, and this life is in his Son.'

"Therefore, my brethren, seeing God our Father hath sent to us, damnable traitors, a pardon from heaven, with all the promises of the gospel, and also hath sealed the certainty of it with the heart-blood of his dear Son, let us not be daunted, though our enemies with terrible voices do bring our former life ever so often into our remembrance."

In disgust, I placed my hat back upon my head, tipping it to its proper angle. Thereupon, I shook the dust from off my feet at the man, metaphorically speaking, that is, a metaphor I had heard John himself use. In turbulent times such as these, what kind of a man delivers a public sermon all about treason, enemies, traitors, execution of offenders, and what not? What kind of a man does that?

30

Bishop Bunyan

On the afternoon of October 17, 1660, all Bedford—rich and poor, high and low—lined the High Street. There was merrymaking aplenty by the children, shouting and laughing, dogs barking. Notices had been plastered about the town that there would be great fanfare and a parade passing through our town on this day.

I stood at the corner of where Silver Street crosses the High Street, the county jail at my back, wondering what it all meant. Suddenly there was a great volley of cannon fire. Clamping my hands at my ears, I felt that old gut lurching of my insides at the roar of those cannons. After our experience in the war, I was never able to derive pleasure from the firing of cannon, even the celebratory firing thereof. To my remembrance, cannon fire meant only one thing: dismemberment, blood, the rending of human flesh, the wanton destruction of lives and property ripped asunder by the explosive force of cannon fire.

I blinked back the bitter smarting in the eyes that comes with cannon fire. Through the clouds of blue smoke now choking the corridor of the street, emerged the entourage of some high-ranking individual. I watched as the horses parted the cannon smoke, tendrils swirling in the wake of each horse.

The men at arms mounted on those animals wore the breastplate, gauntlets, and helms of the Royalist party, swords and pistols at their hips, some with pikes held aloft and bearing the colors of their general, as I assumed it must be. I knew Royalist accoutrements of war very well indeed. For a troubling instant, I feared that King Charles had suspended his promise of amnesty for Parliamentary soldiers, and my heart nearly stopped at the consideration thereof.

After the mounted escort had passed, an open carriage drawn by a handsome team of six great horses, came into view. I expected to see a military man, a general, surely one of King Charles' military favorites on display for the further securing of his royal power over the realm.

But the man standing in the open carriage was no general, no military man at all. He wore an elaborately decorated vestment hanging from his shoulders, a gold-gilded, popish miter upon his head, and he held a shepherd's crook in his hand, also gold-gilded, like no real shepherd would carry about the countryside for the tending of his flock.

My gut lurched again as volleys of musket fire rumbled through the streets, and another cloud of gunpowder smoke filled the air.

Appearing through the blue cloud, a mounted herald, with booming voice, announced the man. "His Most Reverend Excellency, Robert Sanderson, Bishop of Lincoln!"

I had heretofore made every attempt to stand aloof from the political changes afoot in these days. I had tried to rationalize my neutrality by appealing to my profession as jailer, but I do believe it was more from a sense of utter bewilderment from the intricacies of the factions. Put bluntly, I don't believe I understood either party, neither the Anglican Royalists nor the Puritan nonconformists like John Bunyan. I took a measure of pride in being the complete man in the middle: dispassionate, unbiased, able to do my duty without being overly nudged either direction. I say, this was my private posture, but the times being what they were, I was duty bound to make public obeisance to the Anglican hierarchy and the monarchy; and so I did, all the while, feeling smug that I was not overly enthralled with either faction.

Having said that, even I felt a sickening in my stomach at the popish spectacle of the man parading himself like a conquering general, passing before me, before my jail, on the streets of my town. And I feared it boded ill, as events would prove.

I must not have been alone, for suddenly from the crowd, booming above the noise of the herald, I heard voices crying out.

"Away with thee!"

"We already have a bishop!" cried another.

If I had felt sick at my stomach before this, I was at death's door with dread at what I heard next.

"Bishop Bunyan! Bishop Bunyan!"

Others took up the chant. Within seconds, the streets rang with the cry:

"Bishop Bunyan! Bishop Bunyan!"

31

Arrest and Trial

Bedford was to learn that the new bishop was made of sterner stuff, as the saying goes, and did not take kindly to being shouted down in the streets in the very moment of his triumph.

Within the week, His Most Reverend Excellency, Robert Sanderson, Bishop of Lincoln, installed handpicked Royalist vicars in the churches of Bedford, including St. John's parish church. Many local folks referred to these new vicars as "time-serving popish priests," so I heard them do on the streets.

The bishop's retaliations meant that John Bunyan and all dissenters, any parson who would not conform to the bishop and the Anglican Prayer Book, were ousted from their pulpits. It also meant that the congregation of St. John's was now without a building in which to gather on the Lord's Day.

More trouble was brewing. Things happened rapidly after that. I tried to keep my head down in these days. It seemed the prudent thing to do.

But not to the likes of John Bunyan. I wondered at times if he took some perverted pleasure in defying of the monarch and the bishop in these matters. Would not a prudent man simply comply, submit to ruling authorities, not be over-particular about matters of conscience? Would not a family man, for the sake of his wife and children, be able to calculate costs, set aside his overly fine-tuned scruples, and swear the oath to the monarch and the bishops, and be done with it? It made perfect sense to me, but not to John Bunyan, as I shall demonstrate in my account of what immediately followed.

It was not possible for "Bishop Bunyan," as he had come to be affectionately called by local folks, to avoid coming under the close scrutiny of the Royalist magistrates in our community—men I had come to know very well in my profession, I being always surrounded by magistrates, arrests, trials, chains, and prison, as I have said. Hence, I took it upon myself to urge him to keep his head down.

"Low in the hole, John," said I, "as we learned in the war. This is not the time for you to strut about the countryside, preaching from the tree tops."

He laughed. "Tree tops? I was very far from the top of that great oak in Lower Sampsell, as you well know."

"And you surely know that the locals have given that ancient tree a new name?"

"Have they, indeed?"

"'Bunyan oak,' it is called, by everyone now. And you heard and saw the common folk chanting 'Bishop Bunyan' in the streets while the new bishop was parading by. John, you must be cautious. This would be a very judicious time for you to stick with your calling, your true calling, tinkering. There's ample kettles and pots to mend and no need for you to go stirring the pot with more preaching, *unauthorized* preaching, at that."

He made no promises. But I felt I had executed my duty to warn him, though I was perfectly correct in fearing that he would not heed my warning.

My fears were realized less than a month later, November 12, 1660. In a low thatched farm cottage in the hamlet of Lower Samsell, across the fields from Harlington, but a stone's throw from the Bunyan oak, he did it again. Preached without a license. I was not there, but heard on good authority the details of that unlawful gathering.

Unlike many Bunyan gatherings, this was but a small cluster of local farming folk, with calloused hands and muddy boots, pressed into the kitchen to hear him preach. The events of that day and the next proved to be of such great import for Bunyan and for the community that precise details were taken down and set to remembrance.

The farmer host was anxious, as he had ample reason for being. It was rumored that a warrant for Bunyan's arrest had been issued by the local magistrate.

"Perhaps, we should scatter to the hills," said the farmer, "and reconvene another time."

"No, by no means," replied Bunyan. "I will not stir, neither will I have the meeting dismissed. Come, be of good cheer; let us not be daunted; our cause is good; we need not be ashamed of it, to preach God's Word, even if we suffer for it."

I believed every word of this, for it was exactly what John Bunyan would have said. After reading out his text, the account continued, he began his exhortation.

"A man would be counted a fool to slight a judge, before whom he is to have a trial of his whole estate. How much more so is the trial that we have before God of far greater importance, as it concerns our eternal happiness or misery; and yet, dare we affront him?

"The only way for us to escape that terrible judgment, is to be often passing a sentence of condemnation upon ourselves here, and thereby fleeing to Christ by whose atoning sacrifice, 'there is therefore now no condemnation for those—'"

His words were abruptly cut off by the thundering of a musket butt on the door of the farm house. The village constable and the magistrate's assistant ordered the conventicle immediately to be terminated. "We have a warrant for the arrest of one John Bunyan!"

After calmly saying a few closing words of comfort to his little flock, he was led away, to be detained until the following day when he would be arraigned before local landlord, magistrate, and Justice of the Peace, Francis Wingate.

Meanwhile, word arrived at my place of duty that Bunyan had been taken and would appear before Wingate the next morning. This was not good news for John Bunyan; Francis Wingate was known as an ardent

Royalist and devoted supporter of King Charles and all of his repressive statutes and policies.

At the news, I scowled at the iron-gray clouds and the steady downpour of rain. Why could not John have gone and gotten himself arrested in more seasonable weather? Early next morning, I saddled my horse and rode in the mud and drizzle to Harlington, not certain why or what good I could manage to do. John Bunyan was getting everything he deserved. I could not be rid of him. He was trouble in my youth, and he was trouble in these my wiser years as well. If only he had heeded my counsel.

Soaked to the bone and caked with mud, I was out of sorts with our Bedfordshire climate when I reined in my horse before the gates of Harlington Manor House. I had ridden my steed hard, and she was covered in sweat and more mud than I.

Running my eyes over the country house, I studied its large, double gables rising above the courtyard. Gnarly stalks of wisteria clung to the stonework of the medieval manor house, and had been trained to climb the front wall and stretch their limbs obediently around the leaded window panes.

I had never had occasion to enter the country home of the magistrate at Harlington, and was arriving unannounced and unsummoned. John had taught me in our boyhood capers that when in doubt, "transgress boldly," so he had said and practiced in those days—come to think of it, as he continued practicing in these days.

Handing my reins to a stable boy, I attempted to shake off the mud clinging to my oiled overcoat, and strode boldly, as John had taught me, up to the front door. Whereupon, I gave off my name and position, and asked admittance. To my astonishment, the door was opened to me. Shaking the weather out of the brims of my hat, I hung my drenched outer garments in the entry hall, as I was directed to do by the servant. After straightening my buff coat and collar, I was led into a parlor with a low-beamed ceiling, smaller and far less imposing than I anticipated. An inviting fire crackled on the hearth that made me want to draw close and warm myself in its glow. The end wall surrounding the mantle was paneled in carved oak, darkened with age, the glow of several candles shimmering on the polished paneling.

We were instructed to rise when the magistrate entered his hall, which we did. When Bunyan was led in by the constable, I was glad to see that they had not shackled his hands and ankles.

I have in my profession seen the terror in men's eyes as they stood in the dock awaiting trial and sentencing, and I have heard some men's shameless blubbering and pleading. If he was afraid, Bunyan displayed none of it in his eyes and carriage. Throughout our boyhood, whenever I paused for consideration, which was not often, I imagined it coming to this for John Bunyan. The village lawbreaker in chains awaiting the sentence of a judge—it had seemed inevitable. I wondered how this day would end.

Toying with the powdered ringlets of his wig, Wingate addressed the constable, asking him what treasonous activity he observed upon entering the illegal conventicle at the farm house. "And what did they have in their possession?" he barked.

The constable looked confused. "In their possession, milord?"

"Yes, man! It was an illegal gathering, treasonous. What weapons, man, what subversive materials didst thou discover therein?"

The constable blinked rapidly, as if he were considering fabricating evidence for the satisfaction of the magistrate. He must have thought better of it, for he simply said, "Nothing, milord."

"What!" shouted Wingate. "Give it lip!"

"Nothing, milord," repeated the constable.

Wingate signaled to an assistant to come close. Murmured deliberations followed, but incomprehensible to my ears.

"Read the charges, bailiff," ordered Wingate a moment later.

"Unlawful assembly."

"Grave charges, indeed," said Wingate, the corner of his upper lip arched as he looked with distaste at Bunyan. "What dost thou have to say for thyself, man?"

"I am a humble tinker by trade, milord" said he. "I merely teach the country folk what I myself have been taught of God. To turn from their sins to Christ."

I had done some research on Francis Wingate, enabled by his brother-in-law, he being a barrister in Bedford and known to me, due to my profession. I had learned in short order that this was the first arrest for the lay, country magistrate. Eager as he appeared, I sensed he was not entirely certain how to proceed.

Meanwhile, Bunyan's answer was beginning to sound to my ears like he was warming to another sermon.

Wingate's complexion grew dark; his cheeks puffed out, and his breathing became heavy. Suddenly, the magistrate snatched up his gavel and brought it down with a crack on the table before him.

"I shall break the neck of all such unlawful meetings!" he shouted, rising to his feet, his chair clattering behind him on the polished flagstone floor of the little hall.

"It might be so, milord," said John Bunyan.

The plainness of his reply, and his complete lack of rancor, had the effect of further destabilizing the new magistrate. While Wingate stood opening and closing his mouth but not saying a word, his assistant recovered his chair. The confused magistrate, blinking rapidly, sat down.

What occurred next in that court session, shall always perplex me.

"I shall submit a bond, milord, and stand surety for the immediate release of the accused, upon his promise to appear at the county assize in the new year."

To my horror, I heard my own voice speaking these words, but it was as if they derived from someone else. I shall never be certain where on earth I landed upon the idea. Of course, in my profession, I had heard others submit bonds and stand surety in a court of law. But I was no barrister; a jailor had no standing thus to speak. "Transgress boldly," so Bunyan used to say in our youth. And so, it seemed I had. My thoughts must have simply cobbled together what I had heard in other trials. The larger question in my mind, however, was for what provocation was I sticking out my own neck for the man in the first place? I had no clear answer to that.

While I inwardly cogitated on the folly of my words, worrying that I had just committed myself to chains and prison, the magistrate and his counsel deliberated in guarded tones. I feared the outcome of those deliberations.

I flinched at another crack from the magistrate's gavel.

"On one condition," growled Wingate, not addressing me but John Bunyan himself. "That thou remember who thou art, merely a lowly tinker, and no divine. I shall consider the bond, upon condition that, in the meantime, thou wilt not pretend to preach after thy prating fashion."

I was overjoyed. I am forced to confess, not so much for the benefit that followed for Bunyan and for his wife and children. I was more overjoyed at my success in proposing the bond and surety. It was an added benefit, thus, to have placed Bunyan in my enduring debt, an arrangement that could be of inestimable value in the future.

As I sat inwardly congratulating myself, I heard Bunyan reply to the magistrate.

"A bond with such a condition attached, milord," said he, "is useless to me, for I would surely break the bond at the first opportunity."

A hush fell over the hall at his words. I felt the heat rise in my temples. How dare he look with such disdain on the bond I had risked my own skin proposing?

"Art thou utterly mad?" interrupted the magistrate.

I looked hard at Bunyan. It was a valid question, one I had been asking myself for years.

"Milord, I simply cannot leave off fulfilling my calling," replied Bunyan, "speaking the Word of God wherever I go, and to whomsoever I meet."

After an instant of dead silence at his words, a thrumming and murmuring filled the hall that sounded like a hive of honeybees about to swarm.

The next colliding of Wingate's gavel with his desktop was so vicious that his wig went cockeyed with the blow. Readjusting it on his head, the magistrate's face went the color of a New Model Army tunic.

"Then, thou rogue," said he, his voice trembling with rage, "I sentence thee to three months in Bedford jail."

I readied myself this time. With a flourish, Wingate brought his gavel down with such force that it shattered into splinters.

32

Hill Difficulty

For having just been sentenced to confinement in the county jail, John Bunyan was remarkably chatty on our ride home from Harlington Manor House. For my part, I was broody and silent. I knew the man; better than any other, I knew the man. In our youth there was no one who resented restraint more than John Bunyan, no one who chafed at confinement more than he, no one more afraid of restricted spaces, chains, and shackles of any kind, than he.

I had mused often on the phenomenon, and concluded that Bunyan's calling as tinker, traversing about the countryside, free and itinerant in his manners, never chained to a forge or shop, going here and going there as his whims led him—his entire life had been free of incarceration, bondage, imprisonment of any kind. And here I was leading him off to confinement in a cell the size for keeping a draft horse in. And here he was cheerfully following me to prison. I decided then and there, not only was he a madman, he was a bigger fool than ever I had thought him to be.

"Don't be cross with me, Harry," said he. Deliverance his horse had not come with a saddle, so John often brought his right leg up on the animal's broad back. He was doing it then, leaning comfortably on his knee, looking sideways at me.

"It was a brave deed, Harry, proposing the bond and standing surety for me. I shall never forget it."

"So, why did you refuse it?" I am sure I said the words in a bitter tone, perhaps even a harsh one.

He turned more toward me. "You decide, Harry. Ought not I to obey God rather than man?"

"You could be riding home to your wife and children, to sleep in your own bed. But no. Obstinate as you insist upon being, I have to escort you to a frigid, foul, festering jail cell. Obstinate John Bunyan! Why must you make everything so difficult?"

He did not immediately reply, and we rode on in awkward silence for a quarter of an hour or more. Though the rain had stopped, the road was awash with mud and rose steeply ahead of us. I glanced out of the corner of my eye at him. His head was bobbing in time with his horse's plodding gait, and his red hair swirled above him in the breeze. I watched that daydreaming look come over his features, one I had observed many times before.

"What is, John? I know that look. What mischief are you scheming now?"

He switched legs, his left now drawn up and across the big animal's back, his eyes still fixed on the road climbing before us.

"You've asked me a very important question, Harry. Why must I make things so difficult? 'Tis a good question, my friend, and deserves a good answer."

"Well, what is the answer?"

"You know, Harry, how from time to time I have had a propensity toward the making up of poetry?"

I laughed. "A propensity toward *profane* poetry, if memory serves."

He did not disagree, nor could he. But he cleared his throat and, for his answer, right there on the back of his old horse—I knew it was coming—he gave off a poem.

The hill though high I covet to ascend.
The difficulty will not me offend,
For I perceive the way to life lies here.
Come, pluck up heart; let's neither faint nor fear.
Better, though difficult, the right way to go,
Than wrong, though easy, where the end is woe.

Our horses had been laboring up the road as he disgorged the poem. I marveled at his ability to do that, make up from thin air verses like he had just done, ones that rhymed and made some kind of sense all at the same time.

"Do you understand why—"

I cut him off, almost shouting; I could not help myself. "I understand! I understand that you are a stubborn man, one who thinks he is always right about everything, and every other man is wrong, and one who does not care how many people have to suffer for your infernal being right."

Needless to say, we rode on in silence till we entered the High Street, and I escorted John Bunyan to his cell.

I shall never forget the look in his eyes when I opened the oak door of that dark cell and signaled for him to carry himself with his own two feet into its constricting depths. I'd seen the eyes of a wild rabbit cornered by dogs the instant before the creature was rent asunder by the slavering beasts. Bunyan's eyes were like that, wide, desperate, casting vainly about for some way of escape.

Being as gentle as my calling allowed, I took his elbow and guided him into the restrictive confines of that tiny space. I felt his entire body trembling as I did it. I wished the great iron hinges on the low door had not creaked so ominously as I closed and set the door to its steely latch with a clunk. Through the bars, I murmured a few words I intended to be of comfort to him, then strode back down the narrow corridor to my place near the gate.

Little did I then know, nor did Bunyan, that he would occupy that miniscule cell until little blind Mary was three-and-twenty years of age.

33

Scourge to Satan

Winter is a horrible time to be in prison, I mused, rubbing my hands together vigorously. Alternately, holding them near my candle, and blowing warmth into them with my breath, I felt it so even in my comforts being the jailer—how much worse for those confined under my charge.

And a growing number it was. I was to learn that John Bunyan was not the only stubborn man in the realm who thought he was always right.

The residents of the Bedford County Jail increased week-by-week that winter. And they were not mostly debtors and drunks, vagrants and vagabonds. Some were nonconformist parsons, who, like Bunyan, refused to swear the oath to fornicating Charles II, and refused to stop preaching.

After I confined her husband in his miserable little cell, Elizabeth Bunyan came every day to see him for the first week of his incarceration. It was impossible for me not to observe that his wife had the glow of family expectancy about her. In my generosity, I allowed her to bring him extra rations to supplement the paltry prison food. Most days she arrived carrying a pitcher of bone broth, some hearty rye bread, and whatever else she could spare from the mouths of his four children.

So, I became concerned when for two days she did not come. On the morning of the third day, blind Mary knocked on the prison gate. I opened to her. There was the great muscular bulk of Deliverance standing guard over her, making her seem the more slight and frail.

"Mother is very ill," said she without preamble.

"What is wrong?"

"It is the baby," said she, her face upturned toward mine. "Mister Harry, I've come to take my father to her."

I was speechless. It was simply not possible. *Who does this child think I am? I'm the jailer not the Lord Chancellor.* But how was I to tell a blind, eleven-year-old, little girl that her mother would have to suffer alone? I cast about for a solution. And then it struck.

"Wait here," said I. Taking up my great ring of keys, I strode down the narrow corridor of my prison and halted before the last cell on the left side. "John, your wife has need of you." I whispered in hopes of not being heard by the other prisoners. "She is ill. Mary is at the gate."

His face appeared at the barred opening in the middle of the door. I have never seen a man in more anguish than John was at my words.

"She is ill?" said he. "How ill?"

"I do not know. But I am opening your cell. Follow me to the gate of the prison, then go with Mary to her. But, John, you must come back before dark."

He took my hand in both of his and thanked me with all of his heart, assuring me of his return.

Good as his word, upon his return that night, he told me that Elizabeth had gone into premature labor and was delivered of her child.

"But the poor thing was dead." His voice was strained with grief.

Leading him back to that tomb-like cell that night was one of the hardest duties of my calling as a jailer. The previous hardest duty had been turning the lock on him in that cell in the first place.

In the weeks that followed, Elizabeth regained strength and resumed her daily visits. I managed, unintentionally, of course, to overhear one of their familial discourses together. I did not hear all of what he said, but he must have been speaking to her about praying for him.

"But John," said she, "I so long to do more than pray for you, my beloved husband."

"My dearest, you can do more than pray after you have prayed," said he, his words tender, "but you cannot do more than pray until you have prayed. Pray often, my dearest one, for prayer is a shield to the soul, a sacrifice to God, and a scourge to Satan."

I could not hear her words, as she was generally a soft-spoken woman, but from his answer I can only speculate at her inquiring about what praying actually was. I, ever bemused by praying, had often wondered the same, and so, drew yet closer to hear his reply.

"Prayer is a sincere, sensible, affectionate pouring out of the heart to God, through Christ, in the strength and assistance of the Holy Ghost, for such things as God hath promised, or according to the Word, for the good of the church, with submission, in faith, to the will of God."

"But surely, my beloved," said she, "it would be for the good of the church and your family, we who so need your presence and provision. Surely it must be the will of God to enlarge you from this foul place."

"God has appointed all things, my dearest, including this our suffering. Who suffers, when, and where they suffer—all things are at the will of God and ordered by that gracious will. As the apostle Peter put it, 'Let them that suffer according to the will of God commit the keeping of their souls to him in well doing, as unto a faithful Creator.'"

His words were for several moments interrupted by what sounded like a woman at her wit's end breaking into tears. Smitten with shame at overhearing such emotion, unintended for my ears, I prepared myself to withdraw. But my intention was arrested when he continued.

"The saints are sprinkled by the hand of God here and there, wherever our good and gracious God has appointed, as salt is sprinkled upon meat to keep it from stinking."

I heard a deep indrawing of breath and then a cough.

"There is great need of such in this foul stinking place," said she, having recovered her composure, I could only surmise, from her tone.

"In this place and wherever God has appointed. Elizabeth, my dearest, God has sprinkled us like salt that we may season the earth. Accordingly, where we must now suffer is also appointed for the better confirming of the truth."

"Even here in this stinking prison cell?" said she.

"Even here, my love. Suffering for righteousness' sake, is by the will of God. Hence, God has appointed for John Bunyan to suffer here, for a time, in Bedford Jail. Oh, but it grieves my heart that you my beloved, and our dear children, must also suffer."

"I do wish that your enemies, dear husband, I wish that they would have to suffer for what they have done to you and to us."

"That too, my dear, is according to the sovereign will of our God. No enemy can bring suffering upon a man, my beloved one, when the will of God is otherwise. It is not what enemies will, nor what they are resolved upon, but what God wills, and what God appoints for his own glory."

"But if God appoints suffering and all things," said she, her voice strained with anxiety, "must I not pray, then, for your deliverance?"

I thought hers was a very good question, indeed, and that with it she may have bemused him. I awaited his answer.

"God alone has decreed all things and guides and governs all things according to his will. And he invites us, who do not know the beginning and the end of things, to pray according to his revealed will. Pray you must, my dear one. Prayer is the opener of the heart of God, and a means by which the soul, though empty, is filled. By praying, dear Elizabeth, you can open your heart to God, as to a friend, and obtain fresh testimony of God's friendship to you."

"But what must I pray," said she, "when all I have is tears, no words, only tears?"

"God's own Spirit intercedes for you, my love, with groanings too deep for words. Pray your precious tears."

His voice broke. For an instant there was silence in the cell. Then he resumed.

"Right prayer, my love, bubbles out of the heart when it is overpressed with grief and bitterness, as blood is forced out of the flesh by reason of some heavy burden that lies upon it."

34

Lord Hate-good

In this John Bunyan's cross to bear, I watched closely, waiting for it all to wear off.

Some days, it was his wife who came to him in his cell; other days it was blind Mary. But hardly a day went by when John Bunyan was not attended to in prison by his devoted family.

After being tutored in the craft by one of the lace makers in his congregation, John spent time every morning making tagged thread lace, his wife collecting it from him and selling or trading it at the weekly market along the north side of the river. It was by this means, and the generosity of his flock, that Bunyan made provision for his family's daily needs.

His afternoons he spent praying, preaching, and writing—his poetry, but other things, as I would soon discover. His wife had managed to get his Bible to him and a copy of John Foxe's *Acts and Monuments*, a great tome written a hundred years before and filled with stories of persecuted saints from the past. He was ever fascinated by these tales and ever attempting to share them with me.

Weeks led to months, and still he kept it up. Patience, contentment, diligence, kindness to all. When would he crack?

After three damp and chilly months had passed, in January, 1661, it fell to my duty to escort John Bunyan down the High Street to the north bank of the River Great Ouse, to the southwest corner of St. Paul's churchyard. There stood the Chapel of Herne, a medieval structure used now by the County Assize for a courtroom.

Several of his flock, as he called almost everyone in the region, greeted him warmly and assured him of their faithful praying on his behalf. One would not have thought him to be a common prisoner of the county jail. The manner in which folks hailed him was more like he was a much-cherished son of the town, just returned victorious from a bitter conquest.

Pausing between the two sturdy buttresses on either side of the west door of the chapel, Bunyan blew warmth into his hands, his eyes following the Gothic stonework of what had once been a tall, stained-glass window but was now walled in with masonry, though the delicate chiseling of the tracery higher up still remained visible.

I made to counsel him on how he ought to comport himself before the exalted judges who would rule either for or against him.

"This is not a county landlord hearing his first case and playing the role of magistrate, John," said I. "These are five lords, peers of the realm, wise men, powerful men, men you want to be on your side. Every man of them an avowed devotee of Charles II's rule by divine right, and of his headship over the Church of England. Hence, the path before you today, John, is a simple one. Be demure, defer, desist preaching, and declare loyalty to the king. That's the formula. Do this, John, and you have nothing to fear."

He blew softly into his cupped hands again. "I fear God, Harry. The God who calls and equips the foolish to confound the wise, those who are not to confound those who are, a lowly laboring man to confound their exalted lordships. It is God's way and always has been. No, I fear God, not these robed and wigged judges. They can do nothing to me that God the righteous judge does not approve."

As he spoke to me thus, he smiled at a flock of mourning doves lining the ridgetop of the chapel, cooing softly from their lofty perch.

I despaired of the man, so intent was he on his own condemnation. Taking him firmly by the arm, as was my duty, I led him into the chapel, now arranged as a hall of judgment.

"Look, Harry," said he, whispering the words and nodding upward at the blackened timbers of the ceiling where I saw five or six doves cooing and bobbing down at the proceedings. "They've come to observe and carry the message abroad."

I squeezed his arm, hoping thereby to awaken him to the peril of his situation. "Leave off thinking about infernal birds!" I hissed into his ear. I led him to the carved-oak confines of the judicial dock. I gave him one last, good squeeze of the arm, and I set my eyes upon him in a flinty stare; but I was fearful it would do him little good. I took my place near the door, awaiting with dread the outcome of his trial.

"All rise!" announced the bailiff.

Five men bedecked in judicial robes, and wearing the long flowing wigs of their calling, entered the hall. They strode in dignified pomp to the high bench, the presiding judge, Sir John Kelynge, taking his seat in the middle of the five.

It could not be worse, I mused to myself at the sight. Why did it have to be Kelynge? In judicial circles, he was known as a veritable Lord Hate-good. As events would prove, he would soon after Bunyan's trial be the member of Parliament who would be the principal drafter of the Act of Uniformity of 1662, a diabolical law that would oust 2,000 godly parsons from their pulpits throughout England. He was a man known to be harsh, bad-tempered, indiscreet, insolent, a bully, and a blustering coward. Everyone knew it. Kelynge for judge—nothing could be worse for John Bunyan.

His voice rising in a sing-song monotone, the bailiff read out the charges:

"One John Bunyan, tinker of Elstow, hath devilishly and perniciously abstained from coming to church to hear divine service and is a common upholder of several unlawful meetings and conventicles, to the great disturbance and distraction of the good subjects of this Kingdom, contrary to the laws of our Sovereign Lord, the king."

"What doth thou say, sirrah?" began Kelynge. "Do thou refuse to conform to the prayer book of the Church of England? Speak, man! It is a simple question."

John glanced up at the doves, cleared his throat, and began. "The Scripture saith, milords, it is the Spirit who helpeth our infirmities! For we know not what we should pray for as we ought; but the Spirit himself maketh intercession for us. Mark thee, milords, it doth not say the common prayer book teacheth us how to pray, but the Spirit!"

"What say thee, man?" shouted Kelynge. "The Book of Common Prayer is in no danger! It hath been around since the days of the apostles!"

I am not, nor ever likely to be, a theologian, but even I knew that Kelynge was far out of his depth in saying such nonsense. "Days of the apostles"? Henry VIII's archbishop Thomas Cramner had crafted it but a century ago. Even I knew that.

To my horror, I saw John was making ready his reply. Attempting to capture his attention, I mouthed the words, *John, whatever you do, don't correct the magistrate.*

I should have known better. He was a man possessed with laying fast hold of any opportunity to preach.

"Many in a wording way speak of God," he began, "but right prayer makes God his hope, stay, and all. Right prayer sees nothing substantial, and worth the looking after, but God."

Kelynge and his jurists blinked and stared as he spoke.

"The greatest part of men make no conscience at all of the duty of right prayer; and, as for them that do, it is to be feared that many of them are very great strangers to a sincere, sensible, and affectionate pouring out of their hearts to God. Some men even content themselves with a little lip-labor and bodily exercise, mumbling over a few imaginary prayers."

While he spoke, I held my breath. I knew what he was doing, contrasting what he called right prayer with the imaginary praying, the lip-labor, of many who merely recited by rote from the Book of Common Prayer. I knew this to be a fact, for I was one of them; that much I knew about myself.

"When the affections are indeed engaged in prayer," continued Bunyan, "then, only then, is the whole man engaged, and that in such sort, that the soul will spend itself at nothing rather than go without the thing desired, that is, communion and solace with Christ. And hence it is that the saints have spent their strengths, and lost their lives, rather than go without the blessing."

"You've no business to preach!" Kelynge cut him off, changing his tone to more common address. "What is your authority?"

"Jailer! Take this man back again to prison!"

I roused myself at his words, making my way to the dock.

"In prison you shall lay," continued Kelynge, now addressing John directly, "for three months following. If you do not submit to go to church to hear divine service, and leave your preaching, you must be banished from the realm! If after such banishment you shall return from the colonies and be found in this realm without special license from the king—"

He broke off, glowering at John Bunyan. I knew this to be for dramatic effect, to give greater weight to his final words, which came in a great flurry of shouting, accompanied by the beating of his gavel upon the bench.

"You must stretch from the neck for it!"

Startled by the racket, the doves in the rafters high above took to flight, wingbeats pummeling the air in the hall, darting and cavorting above the five judges and the bench. John and I had often observed this in our youth; when pigeons and the like are suddenly disturbed and take to flight, it is at that moment that they commonly heed the urgings of nature that fall periodically upon their entrails—that is to say, relieve themselves.

To the consternation of the judges, these doves executed what appeared to be an aerial assault upon the great lords of the realm, fairly bombarding them with the foul waste material that had been fomenting inside their audubonorial bowels.

His features red with fury, Kelynge yanked his wig from his bald head; recoiling with revulsion, he attempted to shake the pudding-like waste material from off his fingers.

"Take him away!" he shouted, in a tremulous apocalyptic manner.

John Bunyan, ignoring the disruption brought upon by the birds, attempted to speak. "Sir, as to this matter, I am at a point with you; for if I am out of prison today, I will preach the gospel again tomorrow by the help of God."

Amidst the commotion, I am not certain his words were clearly heard above the din. I took his elbow and we hastily made our retreat from the

Chapel of Herne, doves flitting and fluttering above the medieval edifice at our heels.

Once back to the safety of the county jail, John gripped my hand in his.

"I can truly say, Harry," said he, "I bless the Lord Jesus Christ. My heart he has sweetly refreshed in this my examination and now return to my prison cell."

It was times like these, when I felt that John Bunyan may have been the oddest man who ever lived.

35

Come Rack, Come Rope

When the lilacs first burst into bloom and their rich scent hovered on the April breezes, Paul Cobb, the Clerk to the Justice, arrived at the gate of my prison with a legal warrant, demanding an interview with John Bunyan.

Covering his nose and mouth with a fistful of crushed lilac blossoms, the magistrate followed me down the narrow corridor to Bunyan's cell.

I announced him to Bunyan and turned to leave them.

"Is it safe?" said he, his words muffled in the blossoms, while his eyes darted from the prisoner to me.

"Sir, if he were armed with sword and club," said I, "I would gladly leave my nearest and dearest at his unguarded disposal. You will not find a man more stubborn in his principles than he."

"You are certain, man?"

"You, sir, are safer alone with John Bunyan in his cell," said I, "than at home in your bed at night with your door barred."

After setting the door to its latch, I lingered in the corridor. I justified these intrusions upon the privacy of my prisoners on the basis that I might learn bits and pieces of intelligence that might aid me in keeping of the peace in my realm. I heard the magistrate tell Bunyan, bluntly and without adornment, that if he would give his word not to preach, he would be as free to walk out the door of his cell this very day as the magistrate was himself.

To myself, I inwardly spoke. *Think of your wife and children, man. Nod vigorously, and give your oath not to preach!*

But it was not to be. The tinker thanked him most kindly, but then began quoting something from a man called John Wycliffe.

"'He which leaveth off preaching and hearing the Word of God for fear of excommunication of men—he is already excommunicated of God, and shall in the Day of Judgment be counted a traitor to Christ!' So, did John Wycliffe take his stand 300 years ago, and so—come rack, come rope—shall I."

Shaking my head in my hands, I groaned inwardly at his stubborn words. And why did he have to go and give the magistrate ideas about rack and rope?

Moments later, Paul Cobb bellowed through the iron bars in the door. I enlarged the clerk, scowled at Bunyan, and slammed his cell door harder than was needful for merely setting it to its latch.

In my years as jailer, I had learned a thing or two about the law. Without another trial, wherein evidence of him actually preaching, not merely saying that he was going to preach, without this evidence, he had committed no actual crime. The doing of a crime is the crime. Refusing to make a promise not to do something, in English Common Law, was no crime. Bunyan, however, was not the only stubborn man in the realm. Wingate, Kelynge, and now Cobb, if not hated, deeply resented the stalwart tinker.

Not surprisingly, in celebration of the official coronation of Charles II, April 23, 1661, the newly crowned king, wanting to display a public largess, declared royal clemency for some prisoners. Conspicuously, John Bunyan was not amongst them.

"They freed Barabbas," said I, "but not the Christ. I believe that places you in good company."

When John Bunyan's name was excluded from the list of pardonable offenders, his wife Elizabeth had had enough. She went into action.

Supported by members of the nonconformist chapel, she made her way to far-off London. Dauntless, this intrepid woman, as I learned the story from those who heard it first-hand, managed to get a hearing with peers of the realm from the very House of Lords. It boggles the mind how a humble peasant woman managed to accomplish this.

Elizabeth Bunyan herself was heard with respect and a measure of compassion, and a peer by the name of Lord Barkwood took it upon himself to be her advocate before the House of Lords. But acting as a high court, they deemed it out of their jurisdiction, and refused to rule in the case, deferring it back to the circuit court in Bedford.

Undeterred by this setback, months later, back in Bedford, Elizabeth had a petition drafted on her husband's behalf, laying out all the particulars of his case.

Meanwhile, Sir Matthew Hale, a man of learning and godliness of the old Puritan persuasion, one of the most highly regarded jurists of the day, whom Charles II had appointed as his Lord Chief Justice, read her petition. He then listened to Elizabeth's passionate appeal from her own lips for her beloved husband, and promised to do all that the law would allow him on their behalf. "I will do no less, but I can do no more."

Other circuit judges converged in lordly pomp on Bedford for the Summer Assizes, to hear and rule on local cases at the Swan Chambers near the bridge on the north embankment of the river.

Elizabeth's appeal fell on sympathetic ears with Sir Matthew Hale; however, the staunch Royalists, Justice Twisden and Sir Henry Chester, refused even to read her petition.

Elizabeth Bunyan was not a woman that easily to be dismissed. I witnessed the event with my own eyes as I was walking across the Bedford bridge from my house one morning in early August of 1661. Just as a fine carriage, a coach and four horses, turned off the High Street at Bridge Foot by the Swan Inn, Elizabeth was there waiting at the corner. As the carriage slowed to negotiate the turn, she lobbed a copy of the petition into the open window. It was Justice Twisden's carriage.

Twisden ordered his coachman to halt. Glancing over the petition, he scowled down at the importunate wife out of the open window of his carriage. "John Bunyan is convicted!" he snapped at her. "It is recorded!" With that, he signaled his driver to carry on.

In the days that followed, the circuit court justices convened in the Swan Chamber and began hearing cases.

Elizabeth Bunyan was not finished. Encouraged by the High Sherriff, Edmund Wylde, uninvited, unannounced, and unceremoniously, the valiant woman smoothed her skirts and entered the chamber. Before her sat peers and nobles, judges and justices, bedecked in all the finery of their legal calling. Before them stood a humble, trembling peasant woman.

"Milord!" she cried to Sir Matthew. "I make bold to come once again to your lordship, to know what may be done with my poor, dear husband."

I had by this time made my entrance into the chamber to observe what would come next. Sir Matthew heard Elizabeth Bunyan with the greatest respect and tenderness to her appeal. But his hands were tied. John Bunyan's name had been left off the assize list for the summer circuit court sessions; and, thus, his case was not on the official agenda. One thing was clear: if ever a man wanted to act with compassion over his legal obligations it was Sir Matthew.

"He is convicted!" interrupted Sir Henry Chester gruffly. "It is recorded!"

"Will thy husband leave off unlicensed preaching?" asked Twisden.

"Milord," said she, "he dares not leave off preaching as long as he can speak."

"If so, there is no use talking further of him," said Twisden. "He is self-condemned, doubly convicted."

Elizabeth attempted to explain that her husband merely wanted to live peaceably and provide for his family. "There is need for this, milord, for I have four small children that cannot help themselves, of which one is blind, and we have nothing to live upon but the charity of good people."

"Hast thou four children?" asked Sir Matthew, his tone full of compassion. "Thou art but a young woman to have four children."

"Milord, I am but mother by law to them, having not been married to him yet two full years. Indeed, I was with child when my husband was first apprehended, but being young and unaccustomed to such things, I being slayed at the news, fell into labor, and so continued for eight days, and then was delivered." She paused to compose herself. "But my child died."

In the momentary silenced that followed her words, Sir Matthew murmured, "Alas, poor woman!"

But Twisden received her words with a growl of disdain. "Poor woman, indeed, who hast made her poverty her cloak. Thy husband runneth about the countryside neglecting his true calling in favor of unlawful preaching."

"What is his calling?" asked Sir Matthew.

"A tinker, milord," several voices responded at the same time.

"Yes, and because he is a tinker and a poor man," said Sir Matthew, "therefore, he is despised and cannot have justice."

"Justice!" shouted Twisden. "He is the man who preacheth unjustly!"

"Milord, he preacheth nothing but the Word of God," said Elizabeth.

"He, preach the Word of God?" shouted Twisden, his face now red with fury. "He prowls about the countryside doing harm!"

"No, milord!" said she. "It is not so. God hath owned him, and done much good by him."

"God, say you?" cried Twisden. "John Bunyan's doctrine is the doctrine of the devil!" Provoked by his own shouting, the justice had risen to his feet and strode menacingly toward Bunyan's wife.

Sir Matthew's voice rose above the ruckus. "Strike that woman at your peril!"

"Milord, when the righteous Judge shall appear," cried Elizabeth, "it will be known that my husband's doctrine is not the doctrine of the devil."

Sir Matthew called for the statute book. After consulting it, he said, "I am sorry, woman, that I can do thee no good. God knows I wish I could, but I am equally under and subject to the law. Thou must do one of these three things: either apply thyself to the king, or sue out his pardon, or get a writ of error."

Later, back at John Bunyan's cell, as we gave him an account of the proceedings that day at the Swan Chambers, Elizabeth tearfully lamented the hardheartedness of the justices toward her husband. "What a sad accounting such poor creatures will have to give before the true Judge," said she, "for their cruel opposition to Christ and to his gospel."

John held his wife's hand tenderly, gazing at her with wonder. "Justices are sworn to administer the law, my dear."

"But what are we to do when the law itself is evil?" said she.

"We must pray and seek the day when the king's law more justly accords with God's law."

"And until that day?" said she.

"We suffer patiently, entrusting our souls to the God who judges justly. For my part, I have determined to suffer even until the moss shall grow upon mine eyebrows, rather than thus to violate my faith and principles."

36

A Thousand Calamities

For the next five months, John and his fearless wife did all they could to gain a hearing. They had high hopes that John would be allowed to plead his case in person before the king's justices at the Swan Chamber in Bedford in January, 1662. But all their efforts were thwarted by Clerk to the Justice, Paul Cobb. Resentful of Bunyan's principled stand, he used his influence to make certain that all their appeals were denied.

The case was closed. Bedford County Jail was to be Bunyan's home, and I to be his jailer.

"Who knows," said I, trying to cheer him, "maybe you lie in jail for a purpose, a higher purpose."

At my words, he gave me something very close to one of his withering looks given me so often in our youth. "Harry, you are correct. It is most assuredly for a higher purpose, though we do not know what that purpose may be."

And then a thought suddenly struck. "Your poetry!" said I. "I do wonder if you ought to give yourself more diligently to your poetry."

He frowned at me.

"John, hear me," said I. "I am in earnest. Writing it all down, not just tossing it off into thin air as the fancy falls upon you, but actually putting quill to parchment, it will settle your brains."

I went on to make my case that the very act of forming the words on the page might be healing to what so clearly ailed him. And I assured him that I would go often down to the river and gather quills for him, and as I was able, would put up parchment and ink, as I could afford to.

So it was, one day as I was making my rounds, checking on my prisoners, that I paused at John's cell. Peering in, I saw him, quill in hand, laboring over a parchment. I looked more closely through the bars. If my eyes did not deceive me, there were tears freely falling from his eyes onto that parchment. I hesitated. It seemed a moment too tragic for interruption. But then he heard me.

Composing himself, he said, "Come in, Harry."

And so, I did.

"I see you have been taking my advice in hand."

He nodded.

"It was very good advice, was it not?"

He blew on the ink to help it dry, squinting in the dim light at his own words.

"What have you written?" I asked. "More poetry?"

He shook his head, unable to speak.

"May I read it?"

He hesitated. Then, without a word, he handed me the page, and I read it: "I find myself a man encompassed with infirmities. Parting with my wife and four children hath often been to me in this place, as the peeling of the flesh from the bone, and that not only because I am somewhat too fond of these great mercies, but also because I have often brought to my mind the many hardships, miseries, and wants that my poor family was like to meet with now that I have been taken from them—especially my poor blind child, who lay nearer my heart than all beside.

"Oh, the thought of the hardships my poor blind one might undergo breaks my heart to pieces! Poor child! What sorrows art thou like to have for thy portion in this world! Thou must be beaten, must beg, suffer hunger, cold, nakedness, and a thousand calamities, though I could never endure so much as the wind to blow upon thee. But yet recalling myself, I must venture you all with God, though it goes to the quick to leave you."

For my part, I could not readily trust myself to speak after reading his words. More than ever before, I felt ashamed of berating him as I had done, for calling him careless of his family and what they must suffer for his stubbornness.

When at last I recovered my voice, I asked, "Have you shown this to Elizabeth?"

He shook his head.

"You must."

"In time," said he.

"And, John, you must keep writing. I shall do all I can to supply you with writing materials. It will do you good. As I've said, it will settle your brains. And, who knows, someday it may do others good."

"Who knows?" said he. "God knows. My only concern is for my flock. If writing enables me in my imprisonment to nurture and encourage my family and flock, then I shall write. Unlettered, laboring man that I am, I know no other aspiration."

37

Prison Piper

T he months ground onward, during which Charles II and his Royalist Parliament passed ever more repressive edicts against unlicensed preaching and preachers, both in England and in Scotland. The Act of Uniformity in 1662, stripped 2,000 faithful preachers of their pulpits and filled their churches with the Merry Monarch's favorites—often his philandering, inebriate favorites.

Hence, the number of residents under my charge in Bedford County Jail swelled with each new edict. As did the stench.

As God is my witness, I did the best I could for them, but overcrowding of prisons inevitably leads to under crowding. It is a penitential theory, proven throughout the centuries. Overcrowded prison cells breed disease. Poor food, bad water, inadequate considerations for the removal of human waste—all of these and more cause men to grow ill, to hack and cough with the damp and the cold, to gain nothing by the taking of food but a hasty trip to the bucket, whatever nutrients were in the meager diet going straight through the man and into the bucket.

Eventually men die from the residual effects of overcrowding in the prisons. Hence, overcrowding leads to under crowding as the miserable human condition in bondage achieves equilibrium. It is an inviolable doctrine of my profession, about which I have seriously considered, these being literary times, taking my own advice and writing a book.

There were fully sixty religious dissenters and two other nonconformist parsons held in my cells with Bunyan. The corner of Silver Street and the High Street daily emanated not only smells but sounds for all passersby to hear. A veritable chorus of praying, preaching, and psalm singing emanating from my cells. John Bunyan was ever in the forefront of that preaching.

One morning, I heard a new sound, one I had not heretofore heard. Flute or pipe music, it was, as if someone was playing the recorder. I was confused by the sound. As near as I could make out, by its echoing throughout the narrow corridor, it seemed to come from Bunyan's cell, or thereabouts.

Taking up my keyring, I strode down the corridor to investigate, the heels of my bucket-top boots echoing with my every tread. As I neared the low door of his cell, the flute music suddenly stopped. Peering through the bars in the door—there was Bunyan seated by the narrow shaft of light that, at the midmorning hour, managed to slant its way into his otherwise dark cell. He had his quill in hand, his legs casually crossed, looking at the little window of light as if seeking inspiration for the next line he was to set down on the parchment before him.

"John, did you hear music?"

He turned, squinting at my eyes visible through the bars. "Music? What kind of music did you hear, Harry?"

"Flute, or pipe," said I. "It sounded very sweetly, like recorder music. I felt certain it came from your cell."

"Do come in and have a search, my friend," said he. "I have no secrets. I would offer you a cup of tea, some lovely biscuits, but under the circumstances, I am unable to do so."

Setting the skeleton key into the lock, I turned it, pushing the stout door inward. "Where could it be coming from?" I mused, scanning the little room. There was very little place to hide anything. He had only a three-legged stool, a small rough table, the straw mat upon which he slept at night, and his writing things.

Scanning the cell again, my eyes returned to the stool. Eyeing John, I peered at the stool more closely. One of its legs was smoother than the other two, as if it had been polished by frequent handling. Bending low, I saw them on the inner side, a neat row of holes bored into the leg.

"John?" said I, attempting to look sternly at the prisoner. "Have you vandalized the king's property?"

The innocent expression he was feigning, fell away, and a boyish grin stretched across his features.

"Vandalizing? Never! But I have managed to improve the furniture in my little cell, for the greater benefit of his subjects, I am sure."

Turning the stool over, he twisted the polished leg until it came free. Winking at me, he set the flute to his lips and played me a merry tune. Within moments he was dancing a gigue about his tiny cell as he played.

Watching a grown man, brought to the extremity of prison, as he was, I felt a lump catching at my gorge at the sight of him dancing about his pathetic, little cell. Though, I am forced to say, he footed it well.

I was assaulted with memories of our youth, he coming up with another mad scheme on the instant. Many of them malicious, but some merely playfully mischievous, as with this one. How could a man who once hated restraint of any kind and degree, who was terrified of confined spaces, how could he be so contented in such circumstances?

It was beyond me. And I found it hereafter more difficult to harden myself against him, to dismiss his plight as merely the just consequences of his rebellion against the king and the bishop. As always, John Bunyan ever bewildered and frustrated me. I wanted him simply to be all bad, thereby justifying my confinement of him. He deserved everything he was now paying for, so I wanted to convince myself.

While I mused, thus, the great bell at the entrance of my prison clanged. I left John's cell and walked to the gate. There stood little Mary, her giant draft horse protector looming above the girl.

"Mister Harry, I have brought my father's dinner," said she, showing me the basket looped in her arm.

I greeted her, and then an idea struck. "You must come see your father," said I. "He has a surprise for you."

Once back in his cell, I urged him, "You must play it again for Mary."

"And I shall," said he, planting a kiss onto her cheek.

"Play what, Father?" cried she.

He guided her hands to the legs of his stool, and then explained how the idea had struck him one day, that he could make a pipe from one of the legs to bring cheer to his fellow prisoners.

"You are so very clever, Father," said she, her face aglow with wonder.

"Not everyone agrees, my dear one," said he. "But never mind about that."

"Play it, Father!" said she. "Oh, please, do play it!"

Once again, he brought the makeshift flute to his lips and played a long, clear note, a note that shortly became a new version of the gigue he had played for me a few minutes ago. Soon, he began dancing about his cell to his own piping. Mary cocked her ear, listening to the music and her father's footfalls. Taking hold of the frayed tails of his waistcoat, she laughed and danced merrily at his heels. When at last he finished the tune, he turned and swept blind Mary up in his arms, twirling her like she was the daughter of a princess, her hair billowing behind.

"I love you with all my heart, dearest Father," she murmured in his ear.

He held her tightly for a moment, unable to speak a word, his face blanching with emotion.

38

Key to the Dungeon

I took some pride in the knowledge that it had been I who had urged John Bunyan to attend with more diligence to his writing. Without my encouragement, who knows, the man may have frittered away his time in prison making flutes from the legs of stools, violins from scraps of tin, poetry that vanished into thin air, and other worthless trifles. I felt myself in the important role of patron to his art, did I.

Hence, was I pleased to see John furiously writing one morning, and checked on his progress several times as I did my rounds in the prison. Peering through the horizontal bars on the door of his cell at midday, I called out to him. "John, you've been at it all morning. What are you writing?"

Looking up slowly and squinting toward the door, it took him a moment to recover himself from the enchantment of his own words on the parchment before him.

"Harry, is that you?" said he.

I assured him that it was me, his jailer, none other, doing my duty.

"Come hither, Harry," said he.

I placed the great skeleton key into the lock on his door and entered. The door groaned as I opened and entered his cell.

"Your quill has been busy all morning," said I. "What is it you've managed to write?"

He replied in verse:

I set pen to paper with delight,
And quickly had my thoughts in black and white;
For having now my method by the end,
Still as I pulled, it came; and so, I penned.

"John?" said I, in the chiding tone he had forced me to use with him on numerous occasions. "Did you ink those lines, or merely toss them to the wind?"

He assured me that he had set them down with quill and ink, and held up a page of parchment to prove it. And then he began telling me of a dream he had—he was ever a man for dreaming. He told me of a man called Graceless, a great burden upon his back, leaving his wife and children in the City of Destruction and fleeing the wrath to come.

"Leaving of his wife and children?" said I.

He ignored me, carrying on about Evangelist, the Slough of Despond, the wicket gate, flaming arrows, Mr. Worldly Wiseman, the House of the Interpreter, the man in the iron cage, the wall Salvation, the Cross and place of deliverance, mortal combat with flame-belching Apollyon, vicious lions guarding the entrance to House Beautiful.

I fetched a stool and sat at his side. Studying him in the shaft of sunlight slanting across the parchment in front of us, I feared what I had long dreaded about him; madness had taken hold of him with a vengeance never to be shaken off. I considered fetching the surgeon and having him give John a thorough blood-letting. And I cast about in my mind how I was to tell his wife Elizabeth of his condition.

Meanwhile, his eyes sparkled with wonder at his own tale, and he explained how Graceless' name had been changed to Christian, how he had been mocked and arrested in the town of Vanity Fair, how he had been tried by one Lord Hate-good and a jury of scoundrels with names like Mr. Blindman and Mr. Love-lust, and what not; how his fellow-pilgrim Faithful had been condemned and martyred, and how a new companion named Hopeful had joined him on the King's Highway.

"And then," said he, "Christian and Hopeful follow a cheat named Vain Confidence out of the King's Highway and into the wretched precincts of Giant Despair and the iron bars and gates of Doubting Castle."

I studied him more closely. His face was ruddier than usual, his breath coming as if he had been laboring up a steep hill with his anvil and tools on his back, and his eyes flickered with animation as if he were seeing the story unfold before him. His condition was worse than I feared.

"We shall put in," said he, shuffling through the mound of parchment on the rough planks of his table, "just here where Giant Despair converses with his wife, who tells him to convey the trespassers to the castle yard and 'show them the bones and skulls of those that thou hast already killed; and make them believe, ere a week comes to an end, thou wilt tear them also in pieces, as thou hast done their fellows before them.'"

John then explained that, after the giant showed them his bone hill, he beat them severely with his cudgel, and threw them back, bruised and battered in a lamentable condition, into the dungeon. Stopping now and then to strike out a word or add another, he commenced reading from the pages before him:

On Saturday about midnight, they began to pray, and continued in prayer till almost break of day. Now, a little before it was day, good Christian, as one half amazed, brake out into this earnest speech:

"What a fool," quoth he, "am I to lie in a foul-smelling dungeon, when I may as well walk at liberty! I have a key in my bosom called Promise, that will, I am sure, open any lock in Doubting Castle."

Then said Hopeful, "That is good news, good brother: pluck it out of thy bosom, and try."

Then Christian pulled it out of his bosom, and began to try at the dungeon door, whose bolt, as he turned the key, gave back, and the door flew open with ease, and Christian and Hopeful both came out. Then he went to the outward door that leads into the castle yard, and with his key opened that door also. After, he went to the iron gate, for that must be opened too; but that lock went exceedingly hard, yet the key did open it. Then they thrust open the gate to make their escape with speed; but that gate, as it opened, made such a creaking, that it waked Giant Despair who, hastily rising to pursue his prisoners, felt his limbs to fail; for his fits took him again, so that he could by no means go after them. Then they went on, and came to the King's Highway again, and so were safe because they were out of Giant Despair's rule.

Abruptly Bunyan broke off from his reading, staring at me. "Well, what do you think?" said he.

I weighed my words carefully, twirling my great ring of keys about my fingers. "Might you be employing," said I, "the literary device of metaphor—here, a rather literal metaphor?"

He seemed bewildered at my words, staring back at me expectantly. I studied the keys jangling in my fist, then back at his face. From keys to his intense eyes, then back again.

"John, hear me," said I, knowing and dreading what I was about to say. "I mean to leave your cell ajar, that is to say, unlocked, and to turn my face the other way as you walk out of the county jail onto Silver Street. But two things you must promise me. Wear your broad brim pulled down well over your eyes, to conceal your identity, and you must return before dark. Do I have your word, John?"

At my words, he stared at me with astonishment. As his understanding seized hold of the implication of them, he looked sideways at me, his head bobbing up and down, a boyish grin stretching across his ruddy face.

"It'll be like old times," said he, looking this way and that. "You and me, Harry, having larks together about the countryside."

"Not you and me," I hastened to correct him. "If word gets out that I've done it, I could lose my situation—and end up in yours! I'll not even pretend to tell you not to preach, for I know you will. You do so under my very nose here in the prison."

He nodded. "That I do, Harry, every day. You know why I do it."

I broke in, fending off his words with my hands. "I do. Ever the rebel, you believe you are commissioned by God to do it not by the king, not by the bishop, but by God. I know. If I've heard you say it once, I've heard you say it a thousand times."

"You know me, Harry, for a rebel, a ruffian, a blasphemer with no rival, and so I have been. But there are times when submission to God means rebellion against the king. There are times."

I had ever failed at talking sense into John Bunyan, so I didn't attempt it.

"Do bear it in mind, however," said I, as warily as I could, "that by giving you this measure of liberty, I could be hurling myself into the darkest depths of the castle dungeon you were just reading about. See to it, John Bunyan, for my sake, that you bear it ever so carefully in mind."

39

Plague and Fire

It was shortly after this conversation that rumors began spreading throughout the countryside that another itinerant preacher was on the move.

"If I didn't know otherwise," I overheard one man assert, "I would 'ave thought it was John Bunyan 'is own self."

"Which it could not be," agreed his companion, "for 'e lies bound in the county lock-up, just there."

I knew it was only a matter of time. Word would spread from mouth to mouth until the enemies of John Bunyan heard the news. Believing him safely where he belonged in prison, they would raise the hue and cry at his being free to move about, doing exactly what he ended up in prison for doing in the first place—preaching!

I knew it was only a matter of time. And I believe I knew that it would come back upon my head. After all,

I too was a man under authority. And the authority over me was the magistrates, Wingate, Kelynge, Twisden, and their like—all monstrous haters of John Bunyan, and, for my not restraining him, soon to be of me.

Why I did it, I was never certain. What kind of jailer leaves the cell door and the gate of the county jail ajar letting his most celebrated political prisoner at large to strut about the countryside preaching and prating? It was our past life together, and his infernal winsomeness, that had done it. I had no other answer.

There were even rumors that he was heard and seen preaching under the very nose of the king and his fawning Royalist Parliament in London. I tried not to believe these rumors.

In the spring of 1665, other rumors arrived from London. Starting in the parish of St. Giles-in-the-Fields on the outskirts of the metropolis, the dreaded bubonic plague spread like wildfire throughout the city.

First the dreaded buboes appeared under the armpits of the infected, and then they spread to the private areas between where the legs join the torso of the body. Next there was bleeding from the pores, difficulty breathing, abandonment by loved ones fearful of being infected themselves. Hard on the heels, the victim was devoured in the slavering maw of an agonizing and lonely death.

Meanwhile, the king and his merry court fled to Oxford, and lords and merchants of means did the same, leaving the city to the rats, the fleas, the buboes, and the poor.

To halt the spread, Scotland closed her border with England, allowing no one who spoke like an Englishman to cross. Fairs and markets, workshops and craftsmen's yards throughout the realm, by royal edict, were closed, plunging laboring folks into the classes of the poor, the most vulnerable to the insatiable cravings of the plague.

Upwards of 100,000 people lost their lives in the horrors of that plague. City officials established a bone hill alongside the old City Road for the mass internment of the infected remains of the dead.

"John, I've heard the rumors," said I. "A man very much like John Bunyan in appearance and in his manner of preaching has been heard prating on the street corners of Westminster."

Absently, he glanced from the parchment upon which he wrote, his quill poised. "I rejoice at the news," said he, looking innocently back at me then resuming his writing.

"There's a plague on in London town," said I, raising my voice for effect, "as you well know. I have half a mind, do I, to throw the key to your cell in the river to keep you clear of it."

"Now, Harry," said he, "there's no need for taking of such drastic measures as all of that."

I wanted to remind him what being a prisoner meant. No other prisoner had the privileges that he enjoyed; lock-up in jail was just that, lock-up. Why couldn't he understand that his situation was like no other? Fool that I am, I kept my mouth shut, hoping that for once in the stubborn man's life he would restrain his steps for his health's sake, if for no sake otherwise.

Months passed, in which John Bunyan dutifully behaved himself with making lace for his wife to sell and attending to his writing craft, as I so often urged him to do. Rewarding him for his good conduct, I would from time to time, as was my want, leave his cell door ajar and turn my ever-blind eye at his enlargement about the countryside.

"Your broad brim lower over the eyes, John," I would remind him, demonstrating with my own.

Immediately after one of his enlargements, more rumors rustled in the wind of a man so very like John Bunyan heard preaching here and preaching there, in Stevington, in Ampthill, even in London.

Fool that I was, I knew all the while that his capering about the countryside would eventually come back upon my miserable head.

So, it was no true surprise to me when in September of 1666 he returned from one of his preaching frolics of several days' duration, his face blackened, the red of his eyebrows and hair singed, and his tattered breeches and waistcoat reeking of soot and smoke.

"John!" I cried. "You look like you've been to the underworld and back! What has happened?"

His voice low, and his eyes blank and staring at the flagstone floor of his cell, he told his tale.

"On the morning of September 2, fire broke out in Thomas Farriner's bakehouse in Fish Yard off Pudding Lane, gaining momentum as it burned down Fish Hill; when the blaze reached the oil and tallow stored in dock buildings along the Thames, there was no stopping it. In the hours and days that followed, it would prove to be a conflagration like no other. A powerful east wind blew over the city, spreading the flames from medieval house to house, thatched roofs erupting in flames, the wind taking up the flames and depositing them on more structures, consuming everything in their path: houses, royal buildings, and churches.

"Engulfed by the great fire, the tons of lead on the roof of St. Paul's melted like wax, pouring liquid mayhem into the streets and onto the structure beneath, stained-glass erupting, great blocks of cut stone unseated from their place by the tremendous heat crashing down, leaving destruction and havoc in their wake, the cathedral now a mound of blackened rubble.

"Every able body did what we could, but water from wooden buckets dumped on a conflagration of this proportion was futile, as ineffectual as attempting to empty the Channel with a teaspoon."

He broke off, staring like I had seen him stare after a battle, playing it over again on the tragic theater stage of his mind.

"And what of the people?" said I. "What did they do?"

"Panic, most people panicked," said he. "Crying in terror, they ran for the river, hoping to flee the doomed city by Thames barge. Those who set to work to battle the fire, fared better; their distress fueling their will to fight the blaze."

"How many dead?" I dreaded his answer.

He looked at me. "It is far too early to tell. But it was rumored that many fewer died than could have in such an inferno. Thousands are left homeless—hungry and homeless—as their food supply was destroyed with their homes, and winter coming on."

In the weeks that followed reports on the fire and its aftermath came to our ears in Bedford. Though one-fifth of the city was utterly consumed, only six people suffered death in the flames. And one other, a poor ancient soul, Lucky Hubert he was called. His mind befuddled with age, he confessed to starting the fire. After the old man was swiftly hanged, it was learned that he had not even been in London when it started. Not six, but seven deaths.

Hard on the heels of these reports on the Great Fire, as it was being called, came the news I had long dreaded.

I had been discovered. And I was horrified at the news. I was being indicted for the crime of collaborating with a traitorous prisoner. My benevolent actions as jailer of John Bunyan were being portrayed as me sending him, at my behest, about the countryside raising dissension and insurrection against the king.

These were traitorous offenses. I was overcome with dread. I knew what became of traitors, slow hanging by the neck until dead was the mildest. My offense could carry the penalty of being hanged, drawn, and quartered. Cold sweat broke upon my brow, and I shuddered at the thought.

In my distress, I told John of my indictment, pacing the floor of his cell, pounding my temples in my consternation.

"I would be very happy," said he, "to speak to the magistrate on your behalf."

I halted in my pacing, looking in astonishment at the man. Had he gone entirely daft?

"John, you never managed to speak with success to any magistrate on your *own* behalf! It is precisely because I have been over lenient in the incarceration of John Bunyan that I am in the calamitous state of affairs in which I find myself. Cannot you see that, man? Your testimony would seal my doom!"

40
Maniacal Writing

J ust when I feared that it was hanging, drawing, and quartering for me, the initial rage of the magistrate subsided. I was made to swear that I would not, for love or money, allow John Bunyan so much liberty as to stray from his cell, and I was forced to set it down in writing, sealed with my own name, Harry Wylie. Which I did.

After avoiding prison, as it were, by the skin of my teeth, lock-up meant lock-up for John Bunyan. I did my best for him, but for the last five or six long years of his imprisonment he never left his cell. After a suitable time, I managed to allow him visits from his dear wife and children, though never him out to visit them in all those years.

Every day, he wrote. Vast piles of parchment I ferried to his house on St. Cuthbert's Street. I petitioned Mary to bring along her draft horse

Deliverance and a cart to move the great quantities of parchment that emanated from that tiny prison cell in the Bedford County Jail. And still he wrote.

Smitten at times with regret, I felt that perhaps I had over encouraged his writing, creating him into something of a monster of my own making.

Mind you, doing it had come at a steep price for me. Fool that I was, I had long ago pledged myself to supply him with parchment, quill, and ink, all he ever needed. I believe I had it in my mind that he would fritter away his years in prison absorbed in the making of one modest little book, maybe two. I could not have been more wrong.

I believe he wrote fully nine books whilst in prison under my care, and the beginnings of many others that he completed after his incarceration. I felt at the time that if he continued the ferocious pace of his writing, I would need to take up the farming of geese to supply him with sufficient quills, and plant a wood lot for the making of the parchment, and take up chimney sweeping for the soot to manufacture the prodigious quantities of carbon ink he consumed. If only I had known.

What did he write? Of course, he wrote his poetry, but mostly he labored on books developed from his sermons, sermons on prayer, on the doctrine of law and grace unfolded, on suffering (he knew first-hand of what he wrote on suffering), and finding the grace and patience of Christ in affliction.

In 1666, the same year as the Great Fire of London, he wrote a volume on his own life and called it *Grace Abounding to the Chief of Sinners*. It was a title I thought appropriate, having known him for the blaspheming chief of sinners that he was. It was his doing it that prompted me to set quill to parchment and write my own account of the hobgoblins he encountered on his rebel ways.

More so than his other writing, however, it was his imaginative tales that put a sparkle to his eyes, a quickening to his breath, and a fury to his pen. Most of these he would complete after his residence under my care. They were written as allegories, stories within stories, as he described them: *The Life and Death of Mr. Badman*, *Holy War*, and, I believe his favorite project, *The Pilgrim's Progress*.

I have no idea how many volumes so much parchment gets made into, but it would be a prodigious library of books, in my judgment, requiring the services of a draft horse to carry them about.

41
Filthy Rags

From time to time, throughout those years, when I enquired about John Bunyan's progress and what he was writing, he would read aloud, to me and with me, from his efforts.

One such day, he reminded me of the context, how Hopeful and Christian had evaded Giant Despair using the key of Promise, next how they had been encouraged by the shepherds at the Delectable Mountains, from where they caught a glimpse of the Celestial City. After that, they met Little Faith, were chastened by the Shining One for their folly in listening to the Flatterer, and discoursed with a man called Atheist. Bunyan explained that in the episode he wanted to read with me, Hopeful was telling the story of the conviction of his sins and how it was that he at last got clear of them.

"Read it with me, Harry," said he. "I have managed to set it down dramatic fashion, as in a stage play, in

255

dialogue as a conversation between two friends. I'll be Christian, and you, Harry, will be Hopeful. Read it with me, my friend." He pointed to the line I was to read first. "We shall put in, just here, where Hopeful is telling of his fears," said he:

HOPEFUL. …I thought of myself that I must quickly come to judgment.

CHRISTIAN. And could you at any time with ease get off the guilt of sin, when by any of these ways it came upon you?

HOPEFUL. No, not I; for then they got faster hold of my conscience; and then, if I did but think of going back to sin (though my mind was turned against it,) it would be double torment to me.

CHRISTIAN. And how did you do then?

HOPEFUL. I thought I must endeavor to mend my life; for else, thought I, I am sure to be lost forever.

CHRISTIAN. And did you endeavor to mend?

HOPEFUL. Yes, and fled from not only my sins, but sinful company too, and betook me to religious duties, as praying, reading, weeping for sin, speaking truth to my neighbors, and what not…

CHRISTIAN. And did you think yourself well then?

HOPEFUL. Yes, for a while; but, at the last, my trouble came tumbling upon me again, and that over the neck of all my trying to do right.

CHRISTIAN. How came that about, since you were now doing right, as far as you knew?

HOPEFUL. There were several things brought it upon me; especially such sayings as these: "All our righteousness are as filthy rags." "By the works of the law shall no flesh be made righteous." "When ye shall have done all those things which are commanded you, say, 'We are unprofitable.'" With many more such like.

From whence I began to reason with myself thus: If all my righteousness are filthy rags, if by the deeds of the law no man can be made righteous, and if, when we have done *all*, we are yet unprofitable, then it is but a folly to think of heaven by the law. I further thought thus; If a man runs a hundred pounds into the shopkeeper's debt, and after that shall pay for all that he shall buy; yet his old debt stands still in the book uncrossed; for the which the shopkeeper may sue him, and cast him into prison till he shall pay the debt.

CHRISTIAN. Well, and how did you apply this to yourself?

HOPEFUL. Why, I thought thus with myself: I have by my sins run a great way into God's book, and my now reforming will not pay off that score. Therefore, under all my present trying, how shall I be freed from that punishment that I have brought myself in danger of by my former sins.

CHRISTIAN. A very good application; but pray go on.

HOPEFUL. Another thing that hath troubled me ever since my late turning from sin is, that if I look narrowly into the best of what I do now, I still see sin, new sin, mixing itself with the best of that I do; so that now I am forced to conclude that, notwithstanding my former fond opinion of myself and duties, I have committed sin enough in one duty to send me to hell, though my former life had been faultless.

CHRISTIAN. And what did you do then?

HOPEFUL. Do! I could not tell what to do, till I brake my mind to Faithful; for he and I were well acquainted. And he told me, that unless I could obtain the righteousness of a Man that never had sinned, neither mine own nor all the righteousness of the world could save me...

CHRISTIAN. But did you think that there was such a Man to be found, of whom it might justly be said that he never committed sin?

HOPEFUL. I must confess the words at first sounded strangely; but after a little more talk with him I had full certainty about it.

CHRISTIAN. And did you ask him what Man this was, and how you must be made righteous by him?

HOPEFUL. Yes, and he told me it was the Lord Jesus, that dwelleth on the right hand of the Most High. And thus, said he, you must be made right by him, even by trusting what he hath done by himself in the days of his flesh, and suffered when he did hang on the tree.

I asked him further, how that Man's righteousness could be of that power to help another before God? And he told me he was the mighty God, and did what he did, and died the death also, not for himself, but for me; to whom his doings, and the worthiness of them, should be given if I believed on him.

CHRISTIAN. And what did you do then?

HOPEFUL. I made my objections against my believing, for that I thought he was not willing to save me.

CHRISTIAN. And what said Faithful to you then?

HOPEFUL. He bid me go to him and see. Then I said it was too much for me to ask for. But he said No, for I was invited to come. Then he gave me a book of Jesus' own writing to encourage me the more freely to come; and he said concerning that book, that every word and letter thereof stood firmer than heaven and earth.

Then I asked him what I must do when I came; and he told me I must entreat on my knees, with all my heart and soul, the Father to reveal him to me. Then I asked him further how I must make my prayer to him; and he said, go, and thou shalt find him upon a mercy-seat, where he sits all the year long to give pardon and forgiveness to them that come.

I told him that I knew not what to say when I came; and he bid me say to this effect: God be merciful to me a sinner, and make me to know and believe in Jesus Christ; for I see that if his righteousness had not been, or I have not faith in that righteousness, I am utterly cast away.

Lord, I have heard that thou art a merciful God, and hast given thy Son Jesus Christ to be the Savior of the world; and, moreover, that thou art willing to bestow him upon such a poor sinner as I am. And I am a sinner indeed. Lord, take therefore this opportunity, and show thy grace in the salvation of my soul, through thy Son Jesus Christ. Amen.

CHRISTIAN. And did you do as you were bidden?

HOPEFUL. Yes, over, and over, and over.

CHRISTIAN. And did the Father show his Son to you?

HOPEFUL. Not at the first, nor second, nor third, nor fourth, nor fifth; no, nor at the sixth time neither.

CHRISTIAN. What did you do then?

HOPEFUL. What! Why, I could not tell what to do.

CHRISTIAN. Had you no thoughts of leaving off praying?

HOPEFUL. Yes; a hundred times twice told.

CHRISTIAN. And what was the reason you did not?

HOPEFUL. I believed that that was true which had been told me; to wit, that without the righteousness of this Christ, all the world could not save me; and therefore, thought I with myself, if I leave off I die, and I can but die at the throne of grace. And withal, this came into my mind: "Though it tarry, wait for it; because it will surely come, it will not tarry." So, I continued praying until the Father showed me his Son.

CHRISTIAN. And how was he shown unto you?

HOPEFUL. I did not see him with my bodily eyes, but with the eyes of my heart, and thus it was: One day I was very sad, I think sadder than at any one time in my life; and this sadness was through a fresh sight of the greatness and vileness of my sins. And, as I was then looking for nothing but hell and the everlasting loss of my soul, suddenly, as I thought, I saw the Lord Jesus look down from heaven upon me, and saying, "Believe on the Lord Jesus Christ, and thou shalt be saved."

But I replied, "Lord, I am a great, a very great sinner." And he answered, "My grace is sufficient for thee." Then I said, "But, Lord, what is believing?" And then I saw from that saying, "He that cometh to me shall never hunger, and he that believeth on me shall never thirst," that believing and coming was all one; and that he that came, that is, ran out in his heart and desire after salvation by Christ, he indeed believed in Christ.

Then the water stood in mine eyes, and I asked further, "But, Lord, may such a great sinner as I am be indeed accepted of thee, and be saved by thee?" and I heard him say, "And him that cometh to me I will in no wise cast out." Then said I, "But how Lord, must I consider of thee in my coming to thee, that my faith may be placed aright upon thee?"

Then he said, "Christ Jesus came into the world to save sinners. He is the end of the law for righteousness to everyone that believes. He died for our sins, and rose again for our righteousness. He loved us, and washed us from our sins in his own blood. He is Mediator between God and us. He ever liveth to plead for us."

From all which I gathered that I must look for righteousness in his person, and for satisfaction for my sins by his blood; that what he did in obedience to his Father's law, and in submitting to the penalty thereof, was not for himself, but for him that will accept it for his salvation, and be thankful.

And now was my heart full of joy, mine eyes full of tears, and mine affections running over with love to the name, people, and ways of Jesus Christ.

261

CHRISTIAN. This was a revelation of Christ to your soul indeed. But tell me particularly what effect this had upon your spirit.

HOPEFUL. It made me see that all the world, notwithstanding all the righteousness thereof, is in a state of condemnation. It made me see that God the Father, though he be just, can justly forgive the coming sinner.

It made me greatly ashamed of the vileness of my former life, and confounded me with the sense of my own ignorance; for there never came thought into my heart before now, that showed me so the beauty of Jesus Christ. It made me love a holy life, and long to do something for the honor and glory of the name of the Lord Jesus.

Yea, I thought that had I now a thousand gallons of blood in my body, I could spill it all for the sake of the Lord Jesus.

42

Deliverance

Though somewhat moved by reading with my prisoner, I was confused by Hopeful's deep sense of the vileness of his sins. He didn't seem all that bad to me. And that bit about his former fond opinion of himself and his duties, and him thinking he had committed sin enough in one duty to send him to hell, that was beyond me, as was the part about spilling the thousand gallons of blood. Nevertheless, I managed to say encouraging things to Bunyan about his writing efforts. And we read aloud together like this from time to time over the years of his imprisonment.

There was never a happier day on St. Cuthbert's Street in Bedford than May 17, 1672. After twelve long years in the county jail, John Bunyan was released, declared a free man, free to return to his beloved wife Elizabeth, his blind daughter Mary, now three-and-twenty years of age, his daughter Elizabeth, and his sons John and Thomas.

In a great legal irony, the king had issued a Declaration of Indulgence for religious nonconformists, especially intended to prepare the way for Roman Catholicism eventually to be made the authorized religion of the United Kingdom. The release of John Bunyan and many others like him was a necessary legal evil, a begrudging means by which the king and his Privy Council could enlarge the many Roman Catholic nonconformists held in prisons throughout the realm.

Troubles for Puritans, and especially for Scottish Covenanters, were far from over. But for the time being, John Bunyan was a free man.

What did he do with that freedom? He spent large amounts of time with his dear family, singing, laughing, embracing, and eating. His sons John and Thomas had taken over the tinker trade, thereby providing for the family, and freeing their father to fulfill his calling as a preacher, a preacher who also continued writing books.

I was astonished to see how renowned my boyhood friend had become, even in high places. The tinker and former convict, was called on to preach in the great halls of learning in Cambridge and Oxford. The foremost scholar in the realm, Puritan John Owen, the John Calvin of England, befriended unlettered Bunyan, inviting him to preach in his own pulpit.

Word is, that when King Charles II learned of Owen's high regard for the tinker and wondered that a man of such intellectual stature as Owen would go out of his way to hear the ignorant tinker "prate," Owen replied, "Your Majesty, I would give all the learning I possess to be able to prate as the tinker prates."

When Owen, author of more than thirty books, sat down and read the manuscript of *The Pilgrim's Progress*, with John Bunyan's permission, he immediately delivered it to his publisher Nathanael Ponder at the sign of the Peacock in the Poultry near Cornhill, London. In 1678, the mound of Bunyan's parchments came out the other end bound together as a book.

I confess to a measure of envy at my prisoner's immediate and incalculable success as a published author, and had no way of foreseeing the enduring literary legacy of the low-born, blaspheming scoundrel, village ruffian—and he a mere tinker, an outlaw, a convict. Then and there, I decided the world was being turned upside down. The last had become first, and I resented him for it. At the first, that is.

Then I recalled my role as literary encourager and benefactor—his patron, as it were. I indulged myself in the fancy of basking in the faint afterglow of the resplendent acclaim that surrounded him.

And then I saw him coming down the High Street, riding on the broad back of Deliverance. It turns out, the great draft horse was much younger than he had appeared when confiscated for debts by the assize, and bequeathed by my benevolence to John Bunyan those many years ago. Under the loving ministrations of Mary, the grand beast had thrived. Now in his mature years, he raised his great hooves with ponderous dignity as he carried John Bunyan about the countryside, now clip-clopping on the set stones on the High Street directly toward me.

"Greetings, John Bunyan," I called from my settled situation where the High Street crossed Silver Street.

He returned the greeting warmly, reining in Deliverance.

"Where are you off to, John?" said I.

"I must go to Jesus," said he, crossing his left leg over the wide back of the gentle beast. "I have long had the sentence of death upon me, Harry, as you well know."

"I merely meant," I stammered, "to enquire about your travels."

"Oh, I go to the city of Reading," said he, "to unite, God willing, a wayward son with his father. And you, Harry, where are you in your pilgrim travels?"

I knew what he meant, always making an allegory of everything. Could he not just once leave off preaching? I glanced up at the iron clouds glowering overhead.

"Have a care, John," said I, ignoring his question. "There's a tempest brewing. Keep your broad brim snug about your pate. And, mind you, don't catch a chill. Off you go. Safe travels to Reading and home again."

Little did I know that it would be the last time I would see him, speak with him, hear his voice. There was, indeed, a tempest. In the prodigious rainfall, John Bunyan did exactly what I told him not to do. He caught a chill. He was ever ignoring my counsel.

Word is, he preached in Mr. Gammon's meeting house near Whitechapel, London, August 19, 1688. A fortnight later, August 31, the man died in London.

I felt numb at the news, and my heart ached in my bosom. I could still see him, that dreaming, faraway look coming over him as he imagined a new caper, a new poem, a new allegory, or as he laid hold of a new morsel of truth in his beloved Bible.

Being a nonconformist, he could not be buried in consecrated ground in an Anglican churchyard, so they buried his remains on the bone hill with the plague victims and other outcasts in Bunhill Fields on the old City Road.

I managed to get a printed copy of his last sermon, and as I read by candlelight at my table in the prison, I could hear in every phrase his voice, his inflections, his boundless enthusiasm, his bleeding of the Bible.

I heard and felt the wonder in his voice as he read out his text from the Word of God: "But as many as received him, to them gave he power to become the sons of God, even to them that believe on his name: Which were born, not of blood, nor of the will of the flesh, nor of the will of man, but of God."

I cannot explain what came over me, but I wetted the pamphlet with my tears as I read that sermon and heard John Bunyan's voice from the grave in every word.

"Are you brought out of the dark dungeon of this world into Christ?"

There he was, doing it again. I felt certain he was speaking with me, Harry Wylie, in mind when he said those words.

Next day, as I walked with heavy tread from my home to my duties at the county jail, my attention was arrested by a vender hawking his wares on the High Street.

"Pots to mend, knives to grind—any work for the tinker?"

Abruptly, I halted in my stride, a great lump forming in my gorge. Composing myself with effort, I approached the young John Bunyan, son of the same name, now the village tinker, and asked him if he would be so kind as to make me a little tin box. "The size for securing these parchments in." I showed him my manuscript.

The next day, young John came by the prison.

"I've managed to finish thy tin box, Mister Harry," said he. "When thou art ready, I can set the lid in place with rivets. When thou art ready."

Dipping my quill in the inkpot, I scrawled these final lines: I was wrong. Men do change. The blasphemer John Bunyan was changed. He was brought out of the dark dungeon of the world into Christ. He was born of God. He became a son of God.

THE END

TIMELINE

1620 – Pilgrim Fathers come to America

1628 – November, birth of John Bunyan

1630 – Massachusetts Bay Colony

1638 – National Covenant signed in Scotland

1640 – Bay Psalm Book published in New England

1642 – Westminster Assembly convenes

1643 – Solemn League and Covenant signed

1644 – Death of Bunyan's mother and sister

1644 – Bunyan enlists in Parliamentary Army

1645 – June 14, Battle of Naseby

1648 – Bunyan's first marriage

1649 – Beheading of Charles I

1650 – Birth of Bunyan's blind daughter Mary

1658 – Death of Oliver Cromwell

1659 – Death of Bunyan's first wife

1660 – November 12, Bunyan arrested

1661 – April 23, Charles II crowned

1662 – Act of Uniformity

1662 – August 19, death of Blaise Pascal

1665 – Great Plague in London

1666 – September 2, Great Fire of London

1666 – November 28, Battle of Rullion Green

1672 – May 17, Bunyan released from prison

1674 – July 17, birth of hymn writer Isaac Watts

1678 – February 18, *The Pilgrim's Progress*

1679 – June 1, Battle of Drumclog

1679 – June 22, Battle of Bothwell Brig

1683 – August 24, death of John Owen

1685 – Covenanter Killing Time in Scotland

1685 – March 31, birth of J. S. Bach

1688 – August 31, death of Bunyan in London

1688 – Glorious Revolution

EXPLANATORY

John Bunyan mentioned his boyhood friend Harry in *Grace Abounding*, but he told us nothing else about him; I have filled in the rest. The episodes with the adder, bell ringing, tip-cat, preaching to the crows, his narrow escape in the war, come from Bunyan's own account. To these, I have added specific details based on my frequent visits to England and knowledge of Bunyan's historical context. Though a poor tinker, Bunyan did ride a horse later on, a horse I have named Deliverance. The episode with the aerial bombardment by doves during one of Bunyan's trials is apocryphal, though birds do take up residence inside historic buildings and churches.

Bunyan scholars don't seem to agree about the exact order and dates when events occurred in his life. Hence, I have taken liberties with the arrangement of some events, especially ones related to his first marriage and his first wife's death. Bunyan wrote his classic autobiography in 1666 while married to his beloved second wife, Elizabeth, which may explain why he wisely chose to include very few details about his marriage to his first wife, not even her name.

I have created Bunyan's voice from his own writings, especially from *The Pilgrims Progress*, 1678; *Holy War*, 1680; *Grace Abounding to the Chief of Sinners*, 1666; *I Will Pray with the Spirit*, 1663; *Seasonable Counsel, or Advice to Sufferers*, 1684; *The Doctrine of Law and Grace Unfolded*, 1659, and others.

ACKNOWLEDGEMENTS

This historical fiction book is the result of many years of teaching about John Bunyan's life and writings, during which I read a number of books about his life. One of the most helpful was an unpublished manuscript written and given to me many years ago by the late Rev. Dr. Ian Malcolm Tait (1918-2013), English minister, Bunyan scholar, and bibliophile. Additionally, I am deeply grateful to my friend John Hinson, Licensed Lay Minister at Elstow Abbey, for his prodigious assistance in writing this book, including his jovial and generous willingness to appear, with considerable adaptations, in the opening chapters. As always, I am profoundly indebted to my faithful advanced-review readers: Tilly Hunter, John Schrupp, James Hakim, Alisa Weis, Robyn Bridges; and, best of all, my mother Mary Jane Bond.

Douglas Bond, father of six, and grandfather of six and counting, is a hymn writer, an award-winning teacher, and author of thirty books of historical fiction, biography, and practical theology, several translated into Dutch, Portuguese, and Korean. He speaks internationally at churches, schools, and conferences, directs the Oxford Creative Writing Master Class, and leads Church history and hymn tours. Find out more at bondbooks.net.

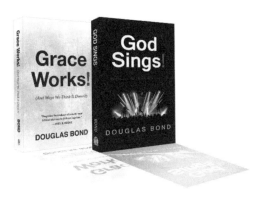

"*God Sings!* is an engaging book that helps attune our hearts and minds to hear the voice of God in Scripture."

JULIA CAMERON, author, Oxford publicist, and Fellow of the Royal Society of Arts

"In *God Sings!*, Douglas Bond provides us with a sure, biblically faithful, and robustly theological guide to thoughtful, God-centered, Christ-exalting, gospel-magnifying praise. In an evangelical world increasingly noted more for triviality than substance, *God Sings!* is a clarion call to the Church to give God the praise of which he alone is worthy."

DR. IAN HAMILTON teaches at Greenville Presbyterian Theological Seminary; and at Westminster PTS, Newcastle, England; and is a Trustee of the Banner of Truth Trust, Edinburgh, Scotland

"Anyone familiar with Douglas Bond's other works will know him as a great storyteller. *Grace Works* is about the greatest story of all: the gospel. Issuing from the faith of a recipient of God's good news and the care of a shepherd, any wounds inflicted here will be those of a friend. Grace is not the enemy of works but the only proper source. It's amazing how many ways we can get that wrong—usually, as Doug argues, by incremental and often imperceptible changes. There is a lot of wisdom in this book, but none greater than the wisdom that Christ is and gives us in his gospel."

MICHAEL HORTON, J. Gresham Machen Professor of Systematic Theology and Apologetics

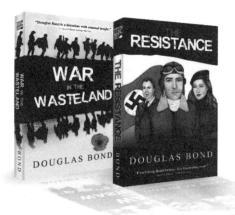

"*War in the Wasteland* is proof positive of what I have known for many years now: Douglas Bond is a great storyteller. Indeed, this novel combines all the attributes of a can't-put-it-down thriller with the intellectual tensions of a historical drama: taut plotting, strong characters, and soaring backdrop. Put this one on the top of your must-read list."

GEORGE GRANT, author, teacher, pastor at Parish Presbyterian Church

"If you enjoy inspirational war stories, flying, intrigue, mystery, and intense anticipation, you will love Douglas Bond's new book *The Resistance*. Not only is the action non-stop, but the thoughtful dialogue throughout the tale keeps you mentally engaged on every page."

DOUGLAS E. LEE, Brigadier General, USA (Ret), President, Chaplain Alliance for Religious Liberty

"*Luther in Love*, a fitting tribute to one of the most fascinating power-couples of the ages! With the skill of a scholar and the sparkle of a bard, Douglas Bond weaves together a thrilling and engaging story."

ERIC LANDRY, Executive Editor, *Modern Reformation*

"If you enjoy reading the fictional works of C. S. Lewis, you will love *The Betrayal*."

BURK PARSONS, editor, *Tabletalk*

"In *The Thunder*, Douglas Bond deftly escorts us into the 16th century world of John Knox. Bond's careful use of language…the seamless flow, rich, vivid picture of Scotland and Reformation. The spiritual aspect of the story richer... A fine work."

LIZ CURTIS HIGGS, best-selling author of the Lowlands of Scotland series

"In *The Revolt*, Douglas Bond uses his unique writing style to produce a highly readable imagining of the travails of John Wycliffe, …a vivid and exciting narrative..."

BOB CRESON, President/CEO, Wycliffe Bible Translators, USA

Neil Perkins, a student at Haltwhistle Grammar School in England, unearths an ancient Roman manuscript. After dedicating himself to studying Latin, he uncovers a story of treachery and betrayal from the 3rd century.

"Enjoyable reading for anyone who likes a gripping, fast-paced adventure story, *Hostage Lands* will especially delight young students of Latin and Roman history."
STARR MEADE, author of *Grandpa's Box*

Half-Saxon, half-Dane, misfit Cynwulf lives apart from the world in a salvaged Viking ship, dreaming of spending his life with the fair Haeddi. When he is accused of murder, he must clear his name before he loses everything to the vengeance of the community that has already rejected him.

"In *Hand of Vengeance* Douglas Bond shines a light on the past in a way that's as entertaining as it is informative."
JANIE B. CHEANEY, senior writer, WORLD magazine

The Crown & Covenant trilogy follows the lives of the M'Kethe family as they endure persecution in 17th century Scotland and later flee to colonial America. Douglas Bond weaves together fictional characters and historical figures from Scottish Covenanting history.

"Will lift you into the 17th century and onto the moorlands of Scotland. This is the danger-zone, inhabited by evil, death, courage, and faith. A story not to be missed."
SINCLAIR FERGUSON, Chancellor's Professor of Systematic Theology at RTS

"Douglas Bond has introduced a new generation to the heroics of the Scottish Covenanters, and he has done it in a delightful way."
LIGON DUNCAN, Chancellor/CEO of Reformed Theological Seminary and the John E. Richards Professor of Systematic and Historical Theology